THE BARI BONES

An Alex Hunt Adventure Thriller

URCELIA TEIXEIRA

Independently Published by Urcelia Teixeira

SPECIAL THANKS

To my three boys,
Noah, Micah and Elijah
May your feet remain planted
and may your lives be full in
Him who have given you life.

It is better to give than to receive
Acts 20:35

Receive a FREE copy of the prequel and see where it all started!

NOT AVAILABLE ANYWHERE ELSE!

Click on image or enter http://download.urcelia.com in your browser

PREFACE

Born circa 270 AD in Myra (present day Turkey), Saint Nicholas, a devout Christian who served as bishop in Myra, lived his modest life as a protector of children and sailors.

For more than seventeen hundred years Santa Claus was believed to be nothing more than a myth—a legendary gift giver among children, invented to entertain the world.

Until the wrong people discovered the truth.

PROLOGUE

1087, THE ADRIATIC SEA

"Man overboard!" The young Italian sailor passed the news down the line to the captain as another giant wave hit the ship. There was no saving him. It was too dark to see anything.

"All hands on deck!" The captain yelled back, moments before another wave washed two more men overboard. The young sailor hooked his feet around the rope beneath his lookout while his hands clung for dear life to the ropes above his head. Under the flashing strikes of the lightning bolts above he managed to keep an eye on the other two ships in their fleet and reported this back to his captain. His teeth chattered under the strain of the icy wind and rain that pounded down hard on his scrawny body. While the captain had noted that a storm of this magnitude wasn't usual so late in the fall, his mother had forewarned him of the unpredictable dangers at sea. Now he wished he had listened to her. But it was a job he couldn't pass on; they needed the money. Not that he had the faintest idea what the job entailed apart from the fact that they were sailing two thousand miles to Myra and back. He had never even been on a ship before—he had told the captain a lie just to get the job. Somehow he suspected the captain knew but had taken a liking to him; or perhaps he just felt sorry for him. In any event, the lookout was an easy enough job—if he could stay alive.

"Is he dead?" the captain asked one of the sailors who had climbed up to the lookout upon seeing the young sailor suspended between the ropes.

"Nah, he's still breathing, Captain. The boy needs his mother's lap, that's all."

"Get him down and make sure he's fed. We're going to need him tonight," the captain bellowed back.

The crew master did as he was instructed and carried the young sailor below deck. When he eventually woke up, a small bowl of cold bone broth and stale bread stood waiting for him. They had survived the storm. Above his head he could hear the crew at work on deck, repairing the damage caused by the tempest.

"Ah, your stomach finally woke you up," the burly crew master suddenly appeared behind him. "Eat up, boy. We have an important job for you tonight. It will earn you an extra week's wages if you can pull it off."

"What's the job?" The young sailor asked between biting off several chunks of bread.

"Oh just you wait and see, boy. Your name will be written in the books. Now eat up and change your clothes. We leave in a few hours."

Barely visible under the pale moonlight, the convoy of small row boats cut through the thick mist that covered the calm water. A small crew of thirty men, spread across three boats, hit the shores of the southern coast of Turkey.

"Come on, boy," one of the more experienced sailors whispered.

The young sailor obeyed his orders and followed the small group of men who silently got out of their boats and made their way along the gravel road into Myra. He was suddenly scared. His instincts told him his job involved breaking some law or other. But an extra week's wages would go far. While his mind fought his inner morality, he followed the men through the quiet dark streets to where they hid behind the trees that surrounded a church. It was deathly quiet and apart from the dim lights inside the church, pitch black around them.

"Ready?" the sailor in charge asked.

The boy nodded. Ready for what he didn't know.

"Give us your best performance. Pretend you are sick until I say otherwise. Got it?"

3

Again the boy nodded. Two priests who had been traveling with them wedged their arms under his armpits, one on either side, lifting his feet off the ground as they dragged him toward the church. The sailor in charge led the way and then hid behind a nearby tree.

"We need help! The boy's very sick," the two priests yelled as their fists hit the church's large wooden doors. It took one more holler before the clergyman on duty appeared and invited them inside. Once inside the sailor in charge barged through the doors and grabbed the clergyman, covering his head with a hood before he tied him up.

"Let's go, boy." He ushered the young sailor toward a closed tomb in the front of the church.

While the two priests stood guard, the sailor in charge produced a thick metal rod from his bag and struck it hard against the marble surface. The young sailor watched in fear as he shattered the smooth marble tomb until there was a hole just about the size of the boy's body.

"Get in!" the sailor in charge ordered.

The boy froze as terror gripped him by the throat. His mother had always warned him not to mess with the dead.

"Go on, boy! We don't have all night. Get in and grab as many bones as you can. Hurry!"

The sailor shoved him toward the tomb offering him no chance to resist. The boy's shaking hand hurriedly blessed himself before he stuck the top half of his body through the hole. A sweet smell filled his nostrils while he continued to pray for protection. He shut his eyes tight as his fingers searched the darkness, squirming when his fingers eventually rested on a cold, hard object. He persuaded himself to reach out and get it over with so he scooped up a large pile of bones and backed out of the hole, depositing more than a dozen skeleton parts into the sailor's bag. He turned to head back in for a second helping but the sailor in charge stopped him. In the distance he heard a noise he couldn't distinguish.

"Let's get out of here! They're coming," his leader yelled as he helped him to his feet.

He ran back to the boat as fast as his cold feet allowed him, his heart pounding in his chest. Behind them a howling mob of Saracens chased after them. Nearing the beach the sailor shouted orders to the crew that had stayed behind, who hurriedly prepared the boats for departure. His feet hit the icy water and two burly sailors yanked him safely into the boat while the crew worked hard behind the oars. By the time the angry Turkish Arabs reached the ocean's edge they had already reached the ship.

Loud cheers roared above his head when his feet hit the ship's deck and they escaped into the darkness of the ocean, back toward Bari.

"What's your name, boy?" the captain said to him next.

"Matteo," the boy answered, his body still shaking with adrenaline.

"Well, Matteo, you just honored your country and the church."

The boy frowned. "How so?"

The captain triumphantly held up the bag of stolen goods.

"Because these, Matteo, are the bones of Saint Nicholas of Myra."

CHAPTER ONE

A nguished screams echoed through the streets of the once small Italian fishermen's village. Amplified by the crisp morning breeze, the shrill cries of panic traveled out toward the ocean leaving in their wake a flurry of fear and chaos throughout the town. Alex and Sam woke as soon as the piercing sounds reached the chartered yacht upon which they had been spending their honeymoon.

"What's going on?" Alex stepped out onto the deck where Sam had already come out to assess the situation.

"Not sure, but something's amiss. I suggest you get some clothes on Mrs. Quinn." He gave her a hurried kiss while slipping on his shoes.

"You're not thinking what I suspect you're thinking, are you?"

Alex didn't need to push her new husband for an answer. She watched him pull his sweater over his head before checking that the guide ropes were still secured to the harbor wall.

"Sam, it's our honeymoon. Can't we just pretend we didn't see or hear anything... just this once?"

"You really think you can go back to bed not knowing why the town is in chaos? I don't think it's something we can ignore even if we try, Alex. You know it as well as I do. Screams like this spell disaster and in a small town where tranquility is the norm, we should at least go see whether we can help out somehow."

Alex knew not to argue with Sam. His instincts took over, still living fiercely by the Hippocratic oath he'd once taken. She knew there was no stopping him when it came to helping people. Besides, he was right. She shared the same conviction. As she took in the chaotic scene that played out across the bustling coastal town in front of them, she could hardly deny her own instincts that gnawed at her insides; part curiosity, part an insatiable need to save the world. She disappeared below deck and reappeared moments later fully clothed and ready to go.

"As pretty as the day I met you," Sam whispered mischievously as they jumped out of the yacht onto the jetty and hurried down the cobbled street toward the source of the screams.

The pair pushed their way through the anguished crowds, forging a trail through the fleeing masses who came running toward them. They were mostly tourists. Alex caught sight of an American flag on a charm dangling from a young girl's backpack. The couple, with their two children, were running away from the front of the line toward them. Taking note of their son's wheelchair, Alex stopped them.

"What's going on? What are you running from?" Alex asked.

The grim-looking man answered in angst. "We're not entirely sure but it has something to do with one of the priests."

"Where?" Sam urged.

"Inside the Basilica di San Nicola," the wife replied and then pointed behind her in its direction, her voice laden with fear.

Alex stared at a long line of people trailing toward the basilica, noticeably undeterred by the event.

"Why are these people all still lining up and not running like you?"

"Isn't it obvious? We're all desperate for the manna. The pilgrimage is only the biggest event of the year, you know. How do you not know that?" Their bratty teenage daughter answered while her fingers fiercely hit the keys of her cell phone.

"Right, thank you," Sam replied, ignoring the teen's rude rant and turning his attention back to her father. "You'd better get your family to safety until things are clear and settled down. Things could get out of hand quickly and it might not be easy to get away in a hurry considering your restrictions."

fresh wave of panicked cries rippled its way down the line toward them, suggesting that something else had happened.

"Hurry, get out of here!" Alex urged the family.

Rushing along the narrow cobbled streets that led from the tranquil harbor to the basilica, they passed several Italian devotees who had fallen to their knees clutching their rosaries in prayer. Fearful expressions lay bare on the faces of hundreds of visitors, some of whom still stood in the long line along the coastal road. As they neared the church further down the street, several men dragged their wives and children to safety away from the church, causing much uproar among those who had chosen to remain in line but instead got bumped out of the way.

When Alex and Sam approached the eleventh century Roman Catholic church that stood proudly in the center of town, a few horrified pilgrims and church clergy hovered over the bludgeoned body of a priest who lay on the steps at the entrance to the church.

Without hesitation, Sam pushed through the anguished group of onlookers.

"Excuse me, I'm a doctor. Let me through." Sam pushed his way to the scene and knelt next to the body, careful not to touch or move too much. His fingers searched the priest's neck for a pulse, but it was already too late. His eyes scanned over the body. Multiple stab wounds across his abdomen and torso revealed the priest had been stabbed to death.

Moments later the paramedics and the Italian police arrived.

"Medico, medico," Sam explained when the police official threatened to arrest him.

It was only when one of the priests confirmed that Sam had rushed to try to help the dead priest that the police let them go and Alex and Sam watched from between the now small crowd of devotees as the police set about securing the area. Inside the taped-off crime scene a police official started his interrogation, fervently scribbling two surviving priests' accounts in his black notebook. Another, seemingly more senior official, did the same with a third priest who was trying to console an altar boy. It was obvious the boy was somehow involved in the ordeal.

Photographers from a local tabloid flashed their cameras across the restless crowd while a few eager reporters set about conducting their own inquiries among the onlookers. Alex spotted the bishop and several more clergy inside the church, concluding that the annual event evidently rendered far more significance than what they were aware of. As the weight of the situation settled over the small crowd of church attendees and pilgrims who stood in terror at the scene, the panic slowly gave way, leaving distraught wailing and subdued murmurs in its place. Several onlookers stood in somber contemplation to one side as they watched the police inspect the priest's lifeless body that lay just outside the church's large wooden doors; his white robe now totally transformed by a large crimson stain across his abdomen.

"Whatever this pilgrimage is about, it's obviously a big deal for the bishop to be here," Sam commented.

"I know, I spotted him too. Any idea what the girl was referring to? She said they're all here for the *manna*."

"No idea, but judging by the number of people here, it must be quite important," Sam replied. "Think the altar boy was with him?"

"Looks that way. He seems pretty shaken up."

Quietly surveying the scene they watched as the altar boy allowed his eyes to wander off into the small crowd that circled him. Seconds later the boy abruptly pointed a shaking finger into the group of onlookers while frantically shouting something in Italian. A shuffling in the crowd where he had indicated summoned the attention of police officers who rushed toward their mark, with the sudden change in circumstances initiating a new wave of panic among the onlookers. Shoved out of the way and to the back of the group, Alex and Sam spotted their target. A tallish male wearing jeans and a black hooded sweatshirt suddenly fled from the scene toward the main street behind the church. Panic followed as the police chased after the man who eventually outran them and disappeared between the multitude of scattering people. With several more policemen deploying in search of the suspect, Alex turned her attention to where a live television crew was filming and reporting on the scene.

"There's nothing more to do here, Alex. The guy's dead. We should let the police handle it. Besides, we have more important things to get back to remember?" he said with a sheepish smile.

But Alex had already moved toward the news crew.

"What is she saying?" Alex asked one of the nearby devotees in the hope that she could gain an English translation. But the distraught middle-aged woman ignored her and instead buried her face deeper in her white lace handkerchief; her knuckles white where she clenched the cross at the end of her rosary.

"You know, curiosity killed the cat," Sam teased.

"I know, I just want to know why all these people were lining up."

"I should have known you wouldn't stop until you find out what this so-called manna is. Come on then. I think that guy might be able to help." Sam pointed to a young male standing amidst a group of apprehensive foreigners who had moved slightly away from the main crowd. As they neared the group, the tour guide's lack of experience was evident as he failed to compose his frazzled group despite making every effort to calm the frantic tourists.

"Tough day at the office, mate?" Sam came to his rescue.

"You can say that again," the man replied with a strong Turkish accent.

"I'm Sam and this is Alex."

"Khalil."

Seizing the welcome break, Khalil stepped away from his group and lit a cigarette, propping one foot up against a wall.

"It's a mess. They're going to take it from my salary if this bunch asks the company for a refund," he continued, clearly annoyed at the unfortunate loss of income he now faced.

"Do you know what all the fuss is about then?"

Khalil took a long drag of his cigarette and stared at the pair through squinted eyes.

"First time to Bari I take it."

"It is, although we haven't really seen much of anything yet. Except of course all this," Alex replied.

"Well it seems you're in for a treat then. It's not every day the bishop visits."

"Why exactly is he here?" Sam asked.

"For the ceremony of course. It's a big deal," Khalil answered.

Neither Sam nor Alex reacted.

"You really don't know? Interesting," Khalil commented.

"We only arrived last night so perhaps you'd enlighten us?" Alex said.

Khalil exhaled a cloud of smoke, forming circles in the air with his mouth.

"I'll tell you for a hundred bucks," he chanced.

CHAPTER TWO

"You've lost your mind. A hundred bucks. Good luck with the tourists, mate," Sam scoffed, and turned in search of someone else who wasn't out to exploit them.

"Okay, fine, fifty bucks and I'll give you a private tour."

The prospect of being inside the church was tempting but Alex and Sam didn't budge and carried on walking. A second later Khalil was at their side with a new offer.

"Look, I just need thirty Euros to even out my losses. It's not my fault the guy got killed. I have mouths to feed."

Alex and Sam stopped and faced the young Turk. Every fiber in her being screamed at the opportunity to skip the line and get inside the church.

"You can get us into the church... today?" Alex clarified with suspicion.

"Yes, there's a back door."

"A back door, into the church," Alex questioned again.

"On my life, yes," Khalil responded with one hand over his heart. "I can get you in."

They took no more convincing.

"Deal," Sam responded, "but you get paid after you get us in."

Khalil took another quick drag before snuffing his cigarette between his thumb and index finger and placing what was left of it back into its packet. He turned swiftly, making a quick call on his cellphone before instructing the group to return to the bus.

"You're getting braver by the day, Alex. Not that I think we'll ever see him again, but okay. I'll give you the benefit of the doubt, though we're not staying longer than what's needed to satisfy your curiosity, agreed?"

"Of course. We're not doing anything other than seeing what all these people are so desperate to see. A little innocent excitement won't hurt. We'll be back on the boat before you know it," she promised.

I n a little over an hour Khalil had somehow managed to get his tour group on their bus, and safely back to their hotel.

"Sam was convinced you weren't going to make good on your deal," Alex commented playfully, with a self-congratulatory tone, when Khalil finally met up with them where they were patiently waiting for him in the appointed coffee shop.

"I am many things, my friends, but I am not a liar. My word is my bond," Khalil responded with surprising solemnity. "We're going to need to hurry before they do the evening mass—IF they do it. But just to be on the safe side, we can't be too careful."

With an enthusiastic bounce in his walk, Khalil led them back to the spectacular church. By now the commotion around the unfortunate incident had quieted down. Bar the crime scene tape that blocked the front entrance, and a small shrine of flowers and lit candles against the one wall, it was as if nothing had ever happened.

"This way." Khalil led them to a small cobbled street that ran behind the sand colored building.

As promised, he did know of a back entrance but it wasn't anything Alex and Sam expected. Instead they followed their self-appointed tour guide into a small shop directly behind the church. Inside, the shop was dark, the lack of windows completely depriving it of any light whatsoever apart from the narrow badly distressed front door that stood only slightly ajar. The strong scent of mothballs filled their nostrils the moment they stepped inside. Sitting snugly in one corner, behind an antiquated Singer sewing machine, was a man similar in appearance to Khalil; visible only in the light from the small desk lamp that illuminated his hands. The shop-keeper jumped to his feet the moment his eyes fell on Khalil, embracing him with vigor. Their lingered greeting and native exchange further confirmed that the two men shared more than just a passing acquaintance.

"Meet my cousin, Yusuf," Khalil introduced him briefly. "We came to Italy together, in search of a better future for our families."

Not allowing any further time for formal introductions he placed his arm around Yusuf's shoulders and turned his cousin around to face the corner. What followed between the two men was a subdued exchange of words in Turkish while Alex and Sam patiently scanned the small, dark tailor's shop. Several minutes later the two men's upbeat conversation had turned into one taking on a more intimate tone which, from where Alex and Sam stood, was now quite visibly a loaded proposal by Khalil to win his family member over. When Khalil finally embraced his cousin and then shook his hand, it was clear his efforts had worked and that they had struck some sort of private deal between them.

"Follow me," Khalil instructed, while his cousin quietly slipped back behind his sewing machine.

Barely visible in the furthest corner of the tiny shop, and partially hidden behind a dusty brown curtain, was a small wooden door built into an arched brick wall. It was blocked off by a bulky wooden tailor's table buried under several large rolls of fabric and clothing patterns. To one side three mannequin torsos further crowded the small poorly-lit space. Khalil leaned across the table and tugged at the brown fabric, allowing it to drop to the floor.

"Help me move the table," he ordered Sam who, upon seeing

the door up close, wasn't at all sure how he was going to fit through the tiny entryway.

With the space already cramped, moving the table made hardly any difference except to allow barely enough space to open the door more than about two feet, just enough for them to slip in behind the table and shuffle sideways through the door. Much to his surprise, Sam made it, and apart from bumping his head against the crossbeam upon entering, found it a lot roomier than initially anticipated once he passed through. On the other side of the door, Khalil switched his cell phone's torch on and led them through near total darkness down a short, narrow corridor until they arrived at a second door. With his silhouette only slightly visible in the darkness, Khalil paused in front of the second door and pinned his ear against the rustic wood. Satisfied their illegal entry presented no threat of discovery, he retrieved a large black key from his pocket and slipped it into the single keyhole. The lock was stiff with age and required a fair amount of force to eventually open, emitting a loud screech through the hollow tunnel behind them. Khalil turned the large rounded doorknob and pulled the heavy door toward them. Their entry point into the front of the church building was obscured by a life-size statue of some early Christian saint, visible under a warm glow of light that washed over their faces. It was only once they moved out from behind it that the full magnificence of the holy dwelling could be appreciated.

"Welcome to the Basilica di San Nicola," Khalil broke the silence, rolling his arms out in a theatrical introduction.

Inside, it was deathly quiet and the ambience was in direct contrast to the cold, damp tailor's shop they had just left. It took a moment for Alex and Sam to respond while they took in the spectacular sight before them.

"I have been in many cathedrals, but this certainly leaves me breathless," Alex finally commented as she stepped out in front of the statue and stood gazing up at the vaulted ceiling, enhanced by a multitude of decorative arches.

Built entirely from limestone the basilica was divided longitudinally into three naves by enormous arched walls and pillars. T-shaped with the transept at the end of the nave, a beautiful hand-carved wooden ceiling covered the central nave, framed by a selection of richly ornate paintings.

"The painter was Carlo Rosa, a local from Bitonto," Khalil declared in a boastful tone intended to impress them. "It's a city just outside of Bari. The locals call it the *City of Olives* because of all the olive groves around it," he continued. "The basilica was originally built in the late eleventh century but then completely restored towards the end of the nineteen-twenties." He walked over to a painting on one of the walls and rubbed the nape of his neck. "I'm supposed to know all the artists' names but I don't. The tourists never ask anyway," Khalil admitted nonchalantly before pointing to the first of two figures who flanked the image of the Mother Mary. "This is Saint John the Evangelist and that one there is Saint Nicholas. He's who all this fuss is about," he added.

Alex frowned. "Why? Who was he?"

"He's THE Saint Nicholas... Santa Claus, Father Christmas or whatever you wish to call him," Khalil answered.

"You're joking, right?" Sam scoffed.

"I don't joke, Sam. He was born around 270 AD in Patara, Lycia. Now it's part of Turkey but back then it was called Myra and part of Greece. Anyway, he lost both his parents when he was a young man and inherited quite a bit of money. Apparently he used his entire inheritance to help the poor and sick. The people loved him. Being a devout Christian he later became the bishop of Myra. My grandfather told me many stories of his good deeds and generosity, but mostly how the Italians stole his body and brought it here, to Bari."

From behind a row of five wooden pews positioned in one of the transepts, the floor-to-ceiling iron cage that closed off the altar in the front of the main nave captured Sam's attention.

"This is a first for me," Sam said as he inspected the black wrought-iron gates.

"Exactly, they're afraid we'll steal him back. He belongs in Turkey, you know," Khalil continued. "Considering he was born and raised there, it's only fair he should have stayed there."

"Wait, you've lost me," Alex stopped him. "What does that have to do with the cage?"

"He's there, inside, buried under the altar." Khalil motioned with his hand before taking a seat on the pew in the front row, stretching his arms out as if he owned the church. "I know you're thinking I'm crazy, but I'm not. His bones are under the floor, enclosed in reinforced concrete blocks—at least most of them. A few years ago the BBC operators in London dropped one of their probes through the floor and they saw the skull in the middle and all his bones spread out around him. They had one of those fancy computers confirm it was him. They found a few more of his bones in Venice and of course the ones that were legally gifted to Russia. Now he's scattered between three countries and everyone is minding their own business just to keep the peace. But it's no secret. They all know he was Turkish."

Sam scratched the back of his head as he gazed at the crypt through the iron gates.

"So you're saying Santa Claus was a real person and all these pilgrims come to see this, his crypt," Sam said puzzled.

"Yes, but it's more than just coming to see it. It's about the manna."

"The food God provided the Israelites when they were stuck in the desert for forty years," Alex responded, eliciting a curious sideways glance from Sam.

"No, not that manna. The holy fluid that seeps from his bones," Khalil corrected her.

"Khalil, you're not making any sense, mate," Sam said as he walked around to the side of the cage.

Khalil rose and joined him. "Somehow the bones of Saint Nicholas secrete some sort of liquid. It's a mystery how it happens, but it's true. Every year on May sixth, hundreds of people travel here from all over the world to watch the bishop tap some out into a glass carafe. The sick come forward, and when they touch it they're instantly healed. It's a miracle. I've seen it with my own eyes," Khalil added.

"So you're saying this liquid has the power to heal people," Alex repeated.

"Exactly," Khalil confirmed.

"Sounds like a tall story to me, my friend, but who am I to argue? What I can't seem to wrap my head around is how the priest ended up dead," Sam commented.

CHAPTER THREE

A sudden hollow noise jerked Alex's attention to the back of the church. Aware that Sam had also heard it they both paused, holding up a finger to Khalil to be quiet. Concluding that it was highly unlikely the church would open for evening mass considering the earlier events, their eyes swiftly scanned each row of the church. Then, amplified by the perfect acoustics, they heard rapid footsteps moving from one end of the church to the other. This time there was no mistaking it. They were not alone.

Khalil had heard the footsteps also and leaped across the floor to hide between the front pews. Alex and Sam took cover behind pillars on either side of the main nave. From behind one of the statues in the back of the church Alex spotted a faint shadow that stretched out across the marble floor. Whoever it was, he was an amateur. Using her hands she signaled the intruder's position to Sam and with Khalil still hiding between the pews, they slowly made their way toward the back of the church. The shadow hadn't moved until the faint squeaking of Sam's rubber soles on the marble floor alerted the intruder that they were closing in on him. The slim figure of a man wearing a black hooded sweater and denim pants dashed across the back of the basilica.

"Stop!" Alex yelled, recognizing him to be the man who'd fled the scene earlier, but he had already disappeared behind a door in the furthermost corner.

"Wait here, Khalil," Sam shouted back, "and stay down!" he added.

With their guns now firmly gripped in their hands—thankful they had managed to sneak them in past the border control—Alex and Sam fell back against the wall on either side of the closed door.

"Think it's the murderer?" Sam whispered to Alex.

"If it is, he'd be looking for whatever he was after, before he killed the priest," Alex whispered back.

"Ready?" Sam asked again. Alex nodded, giving Sam the go-ahead to open the door while she watched his back.

With trained precision Sam opened the door and moved through with Alex closely behind him. With their guns in hand their eyes scanned across the room. It was empty. Built entirely out of large square blocks of stone, the room, resemblant of a small gathering place, was fully illuminated by several yellow and red stained-glass windows. A red Persian rug decorated the otherwise bare stone floor while small statues pointed towards an archway at the far end. With the walls smoothed out and nothing to take cover behind, they were entirely exposed. They remained alert as they moved through the room towards the archway.

"We just want to talk," Alex said in a gentle voice, surprised that it didn't echo through the empty space.

Her invitation was unanswered and they each hid behind a statue on either side of the open doorway. Alex tightened her fingers around her gun's grip and popped her head out from behind the stone structure into the next room. Still she didn't see anyone. Fully alert with their guns stretched out in front of them, they proceeded to cautiously move through the curved entrance. In doing so their eyes immediately drew upward to the roof that had entirely disappeared and made space for a large bell that hung three stories above their heads. The sound of the intruder's feet as they hit the open staircase which spiraled along the outer walls toward the bell, resounded in the tower.

"You've got to be kidding me. Why am I always forced to climb up things?" Alex exclaimed.

"You have a fear of heights and I have a fear of tight spaces. We're the perfect team. I'll go," Sam said playfully, before he headed up the stone steps.

Relieved to stay behind Alex remained gaping up into the bell tower, her eyes and ears pinned to the echoing footsteps of the intruder.

"You have nowhere to go once you reach the top! We just want to talk!" she yelled again. Her words must have had some effect on the man since his footsteps stopped for a brief instance. Seizing the moment she tried again.

"Why are you running away from us? We mean you no harm. Come down so we can talk."

From where she stood she spotted the man where he had paused on the steps halfway up the tower. There was no sign of any weapon.

"We'll put our guns down but you need to come down and talk to us. Whatever you're running away from we can help you," she said again, deciding to trust her gut instinct.

Alex watched as Sam stopped about ten steps away from the man, affording him the opportunity to come to his senses. Alex dropped her gun on the stone floor and kicked it away.

"Now come down. My partner is behind you. Let's talk."

The man turned around in search of Sam and it was then Alex got a full view of his face. She drew in a sharp breath as she realized he wasn't an adult man at all. The frightened eyes of a young boy, probably in his mid-teens, met hers. Desperate for another way out the boy leaned forward against the low railing. Sam paused about five steps behind the boy and kicked his gun down the stairs.

In that moment the unexpected flapping of the resident pigeons in the top of the bell tower bounced off the walls and the frightened boy swung around in panic. His sudden reaction sent him off balance and he slipped backward over the railing. The boy let out a tormented yelp, his hands desperately flailing to take hold of anything to save him from the deadly fall. With her heart caught midway between her throat and her stomach, Alex watched in anguish. Sam's strong hands managed to take hold of the boy's arm—just in time. She leaped up the stairs two steps at a time to where Sam was desperately wrestling against the weight of the boy's body that dangled from his one arm; the youth's other arm still desperately flailing through the air.

Fear lay deep in the boy's green eyes while his feet swung over the gaping space beneath him.

"Hold on! We've got you," Sam said with a strained voice as he tightened his grip around the boy's arm while anchoring himself onto the low railing with his other hand.

"Give me your other hand!" Alex shouted, reaching out over the railing.

The boy briefly looked up into her eyes before looking down at the distant floor.

"Look at me! Don't look down! We've got you! Swing your body up and grab my hand!" Alex urged again, taking note of the fact that Sam's hand had slipped further along the boy's arm towards his hand.

"You can do this! Take my hand!" she yelled again.

This time the boy listened and he flung his free arm up in an attempt to grab Alex's hand. He missed. Sam felt the fabric of the boy's sleeve slip two more inches beneath his grip as the momentum of the maneuver placed additional strain on Sam's already weary arm. The boy let out another emotional scream.

Alex reached out and closed her fist over the fabric of the

boy's sweater behind his neck. Tears ran down the teen's dirty cheeks. Somehow the boy managed to regain control of his arm and gripped onto the sleeve of Alex's leather jacket.

"Good! Now try to pull yourself up with that arm," Alex instructed, hoping it might afford enough relief for Sam to tighten his grip again.

The boy pulled with all his might, but still it wasn't enough and Sam felt the fabric under his hands slip once more. His eyes met those of the young teen's and it was as if the boy instinctively knew this was his end.

"No! Don't give up!" Sam shouted at him.

Fear evaporated from the boy's eyes as Sam fought to hold onto his arm but the slippery fabric continued to slide out from under his grip. Time froze ever so briefly in that moment and the world around them grew silent. There was nothing more either of them could do to save the young teen's life. Sam stared into the boy's eyes, silently apologizing for failing him. It was only when he felt the force of someone pushing against his body that his attention was jerked back into the present. Khalil's hands latched onto the boy's shoulder and with the combined strength of all three of them, they successfully heaved the teen's body over the railing and safely onto the stairwell.

"What took you so long?" Sam said with a quivering voice as Khalil smiled and helped Sam and the boy to their feet.

The teen's olive-toned face was pale with shock and Sam cupped his face with both hands. He smiled as he stared into the boy's eyes and pulled him into his chest.

"You're okay," Sam whispered into the boy's ear. "You're okay."

Still in a state of shock the young man didn't react.

"What's your name?" Sam asked, but the teen didn't answer. Instead he dried his face against one shoulder and wiped his nose on his sleeve.

"It's okay, we'll get you someplace safe and figure things out."

"We need to get out of here, Sam. I'm sure the entire town heard the commotion echo from the tower," Alex prompted, already making her way down the steps, pausing briefly to pick up Sam's gun that had tumbled further down the stairwell.

"Thanks, Khalil. You saved the lad's life." Sam patted their guide on the back as they descended the staircase.

With both guns retrieved and all four of them still recovering from the near fatal incident, they made their way back to the central part of the church building, relieved that the church remained silent and that there was still no sign of life inside. Praying the noise hadn't drawn the attention of the town's people, they hoped they could quietly slip out. But as they approached a row of pews in the right transept, Alex suddenly stopped, silently drawing Sam's attention to the door of the confession box that was open. It had been closed earlier.

Alex and Sam held back. "Go on ahead with the boy Khalil. We'll catch up in a minute," Sam instructed in a low whisper.

Khalil didn't hesitate and ushered the boy toward the secret door. Alex and Sam proceeded with caution, moving between the aisles in the direction of the confession box. The sudden unmistakable sound of a switchblade sliced through the quiet confines inside the basilica.

Hearing this, Khalil pushed the youth down onto the floor between the pews and hunched down next to him. On full alert, Alex and Sam pointed their weapons in the direction of the unexpected sound. With their backs pressed together, obscured between the pillars, their eyes searched ferociously through every corner of the church as they stealthily moved between the aisles.

CHAPTER FOUR

"Perhaps we should just get the boy and Khalil out safely first and then come back," Sam whispered.

"I agree, but not through the secret entrance. We can't put Yusuf in jeopardy. We'll have to leave through the front door," Alex whispered back.

Remaining in their back-to-back formation they slowly retreated to where Khalil and the boy were hiding between the pews. A loud scuffle followed by the sound of a hymn book falling noisily onto the floor sounded from between the pews. Breaking their defense formation Alex and Sam rushed to where they had left them and found Khalil unconscious on the floor. The boy was gone. Another noise drew their attention back toward the direction of the caged crypt. Alex moved toward it with Sam closely on her heels. Illuminated by the overhanging chandelier they spotted the youth, pinned against one of the columns with a glistening blade pressed firmly against his neck. A warning next to the boy's ear was barely audible from where they were. The assailant increased the pressure of the knife against the boy's neck and repeated his threat. With his back toward them he was unaware of their presence. Using it to their advantage, Alex and Sam quietly moved in on them. Within earshot of the assailant's demands there was no mistaking that he was speaking Chinese. Their minds flooded with questions as they moved into position behind the attacker. The frightened boy spotted Sam, his eyes betraying the rescue mission. The assailant, his face entirely concealed by a red mask, spun around and pushed the teen to the floor. The attacker charged forward and thrust his knife at Sam's chest. Quick to react Sam's forearm blocked the attack followed by a swift left hook across the masked man's face. The defense tactic did little to fend off the attacker and he took another stab at Sam's side. With the youth now out of harm's way, Alex took a stance next to Sam, aiming her gun at the attacker, but the man didn't surrender.

"No! Not in a church! No shooting in the church!" Khalil's voice croaked from between the pews behind them, affording the masked man the perfect opportunity to take flight and escape out the front door.

"What were you thinking, Khalil? You just let him get away," Alex yelled in irritation.

Khalil came out into the aisle from behind the pews, rubbing the back of his head where he'd been struck. "I don't care. This is a holy place and I won't allow killing in here."

He didn't wait for a response from Alex and instead hurried toward their secret exit.

"He's right, you know," Sam whispered while planting a gentle kiss on her cheek as he and the boy hastily followed Khalil.

"So you're okay with the fact that the priest's murderer just got away?" Alex trailed through the dark passage behind them, unable to let the topic go. "We almost had him, Sam!"

"I wouldn't lose any sleep over it, Alex. I have a feeling he'll be back. He wanted something from this boy and as long as he's with us, the murderer will come to us, and this time we'll be ready for him; if he is in fact the one who murdered the priest," Sam said calmly as they stepped back inside the tailor's shop.

Sam's comment silenced her. As usual his logic prevailed. There was indeed something more sinister around the boy's involvement.

Once outside, Khalil turned to face Sam. "I believe our transaction is complete."

"Indeed," Sam responded retrieving a few notes from his pocket. "We couldn't have saved the boy's life without you, Khalil." He paused and then continued. "But we can't turn our backs on him now. He's involved in something and clearly he's in over his head. Any chance you'd be keen on earning a little added bonus?" Sam asked.

Khalil shoved the notes into his jacket pocket and pulled out a cigarette. His eyes briefly looked back at Alex and the boy before he took a long drag from his smoke.

"I don't know, man. Things got out of hand in there. I almost got killed, you know. We're talking murdered priests and killers on the loose here. I have a family back home," Khalil added while he anxiously sucked on his cigarette.

"We could really do with your help, Khalil. You clearly know your way around here. For now we just need you to find us a translator. I don't think the boy speaks any English. That's all. Just someone who will translate for us. We'll make sure you're protected."

Khalil grew quiet and turned to the side, staring at his feet. After a small pause he finally spoke again.

"I speak six languages." He crushed the cigarette under his shoe.

"Does that mean you'll help us then?"

Khalil stuck his hands in his pockets and stared at the dried blood stain on the church steps.

"I'm not doing it for you. I'm doing it for the boy and the dead priest."

"Agreed," Sam said quickly as he held out his hand.

A small group of church clergy turned the corner and walked toward the church.

"We should get out of here. The boy's not safe out in the open like this, " Alex cautioned. "Besides, it looks like he hasn't eaten in days. Let's take him back to our boat and see if he'll tell us who is after him. Whoever that guy was, he meant business, and you're right, he's after the boy for some reason.

We're going to need him to talk if we are to have any chance of making sure he doesn't get killed," she added.

Once at their mooring, Khalil paused next to the small luxury yacht and let out a whistle similar to the one a guy makes when he lays eyes on a beautiful girl. "Impressive," he remarked.

"She is, but she's not ours I'm afraid, mate. It's only a rental. As it happens we're on our honeymoon," Sam said as he hopped on deck and started untying the guide ropes.

"You're on your honeymoon. And you're giving it up chasing after a bad guy. Well that's one for the books," Khalil commented, as he followed Alex and the boy down below deck.

"Never thought I'd ever have the privilege of stepping inside one of these. My wife would never believe me." Khalil traced his hands across the white leather sofa while his eyes took in the designer kitchen.

"You're married?" Alex asked, putting a quickly-warmed plate of leftover pasta from the night before in front of the boy.

"Ten years next spring. I have two girls." He pulled his wallet from his jacket and proudly flipped it open to a photo.

Alex stared at the picture of the two young girls on a beach next to their mother. "They're cute. Perhaps they'll join us for dinner tomorrow."

"Oh, they're not here. They're back home, in Turkey."

"Why aren't you with them?"

Khalil shut his wallet abruptly and popped it back inside his jacket pocket without answering, signaling it was a topic he didn't want to discuss any further. He stared out the small window and noticed they had already left the harbor. Realizing it was best not to push him, Alex poured three glasses of wine and placed one in front of him.

"No thanks. I don't drink. I'll take a soda if you have any."

"Of course," Alex responded, quickly removing the glass of wine and replacing it with a can of Coca Cola, depositing a second one in front of the teen.

"I'm sorry for yelling at you earlier," she said, leaning against the countertop in the kitchen. "I'm a sore loser when it comes to keeping criminals off the street and for a moment there I forgot we were in a church."

"That's okay. I can tell you're not used to being in a church that often."

"How do you know?" Alex responded, gulping down a big mouthful of wine.

"Just a hunch."

"And you are; frequently in church?"

"Every Sunday, and if my schedule allows, on a Wednesday too. You should try it sometime. It's the one place the ugliness of the world disappears and you can just be yourself—focus on your soul and the path laid out for you."

Alex shuffled uncomfortably.

"You don't believe?" Khalil remarked.

"Do you?"

"But of course! How can you not? Look around you. How do you think that beautiful sunset was created?" Khalil said, before gulping down several large mouthfuls of soda. "Although, you had me going there for a bit earlier. Your knowledge of the Bible is impressive."

"I agree," Sam interrupted as he made his way down from the deck. "You're my wife and I never knew you knew the Bible that well."

Alex didn't comment. Instead she directed her attention back to Khalil.

"I thought you said you were Turkish. Aren't you meant to follow the Islamic faith?" She probed.

"I'm not like most Turkish. I've been a Christian all my life, as were my father and his father before him. Unfortunately, we're not permitted to freely admit it back home. We're the minority in the country."

"Is that why you left Turkey?" Alex asked with tenderness.

"I suppose you can put it that way. My wife isn't a Christian. She comes from a wealthy Arab family. We got married in secret and managed to keep it hidden from her family for seven years. I still don't know how her father found out but he did. I came home from work one night and he had taken my wife and kids. When I tried to contact them he forbade me to ever set foot near them again. The next thing I knew, I found myself in jail on some bogus charge. Money buys power and I'd still be locked up in jail if it wasn't for Yusuf who somehow made a deal with a crooked *Köy Korucusu,*. It doesn't take much to bribe our police. He managed to sneak me out and get me safely out of the country. I have tried to send letters and stay in contact but I haven't seen or heard from them since."

Khalil's voice trailed off and the atmosphere fell silent until he suddenly perked up and spoke with newfound energy.

"Anyway, such is life. We don't let these things define us. We move on. Much like I suspect this brave boy next to me is trying to do."

"You're right. Let's see if we can find out where he's from and why he's mixed up with the Chinese." Sam took a seat opposite the boy who so far hadn't said a single word.

"What's your name, son?" Sam started.

The boy's big green eyes declared he had no idea what Sam was saying.

Sam pressed his palm onto his chest. "I'm Sam," then pointed to Alex and in turn Khalil, sounding out their names respectively.

A faint smile erupted from the boy's dirty face.

"Stavros," the boy answered between mouthfuls.

"He's Greek," Khalil said with elation, and immediately welcomed the boy in perfectly spoken Greek.

The boy's face lit up resulting in a further quick exchange between Khalil and him.

"What's he saying?" Alex nudged for Khalil to translate.

CHAPTER FIVE

So far he's thanking us for saving his life back at the church.

"Ask him if he's alone and what he's doing here so far from home?" Sam spoke and Khalil promptly translated.

Tears welled up in the boy's eyes before he looked down at his dirty fingers and fiddled with the metal ring of his soda can. Khalil asked him again, this time with more tenderness. Wiping his nose with the back of his hand the boy took a deep breath and started talking, pausing to allow Khalil to translate his story.

"He says he traveled here from Mathraki, a small remote island not far from Corfu. His mother is very ill and the doctors say they can't do anything for her anymore. He came here to get some manna so she can be healed. He never knew his father. She raised him on her own. He is all she has. So he took a ferry to Ag Stephanos and traveled to Corfu by bus before catching a lift with a private sailboat in exchange for washing their diving gear and doing the dishes. They dropped him off in Taranto and then he hitched rides to Bari. But then he got robbed of the money he had saved up to gain entry to the ceremony."

The sad tone of Stavros' voice suddenly became heavy with fear.

"Calm down, lad," Sam consoled, but Stavros paid little attention to him and continued rambling with heightened anxiety.

"Shh, it's okay. We're going to help you," Khalil comforted him.

"What did he say?" Alex enquired when the boy finally calmed down.

"He says he had no choice but to steal the manna from the crypt. So he sneaked into the church just before the ceremony was supposed to start. That's when the altar boy saw him so he ran and took up hiding in the bell tower. He saw the man with the mask come out from behind the pews and the next thing he knew the priest was dead and the police were chasing him."

"Wait, the same masked man from earlier?" Alex probed.

Khalil translated and then replied by nodding his head.

"But he didn't actually see him kill the priest?" Sam asked.

"No, he only heard the screams," Khalil rendered again.

"And what happened to the manna?" Alex asked.

"He doesn't know. That's why he went back again," Khalil continued.

"But of course he couldn't get it because it was behind the iron enclosure. And clearly the masked man doesn't have any either, otherwise he wouldn't be chasing Stavros," Sam reasoned.

Alex paced the tiny space in the kitchen. "We still have a dead priest. He must have taken the manna and tried to protect it."

"What I don't understand is why they're all arguing over it. Why kill the priest over it? Surely he could've just tapped more and given it to the man," Sam said as he got up to pour more wine.

"It doesn't work that way, I'm afraid. The St. Nicholas bones only produce one cup of manna each year, no more and no less. Many have tried tapping more, but with no success. Once it's tapped it only produces again in three hundred and sixty-five days. The ceremony is highly revered in the Catholic church and considered extremely holy," Khalil explained.

"Well, that explains its value then. It is of course entirely possible that the manna isn't actually missing and that it was secured by the bishop and the church, perhaps somewhere off site," Sam ventured as Alex took his place opposite Stavros.

"Poor boy risked life and limb to save his mother's life. Only to go home empty handed and possibly stand wrongfully accused of murdering a priest," Alex added, her voice suddenly burdened. "We can't let that happen, Sam. We have to help this boy. I know first-hand what it's like losing a mother. You're a doctor. I'm sure you can have a look at her. By the sounds of it I doubt his mother could afford proper medical treatment. For all we know she has a bad case of the flu."

Sam sat back in his chair as he contemplated the gravity of the situation then nodded in agreement.

"We'll be aiding in his escape," Khalil intervened.

"He's not guilty. I believe the boy," Sam said.

"We have no proof of that, only his word," Khalil argued.

"Then we'll find proof. We'll hunt down the murderer and prove his innocence," Alex exclaimed. "But first we need to get him home and see what we can do for his mother."

"Then it's agreed. We'll stay put here for the night and set sail at first light," Sam confirmed.

"I'll take the first shift," Alex declared while taking a fresh towel from a nearby cupboard before directing the boy to the bathroom and his cabin.

"First shift. What do you mean?" Khalil uttered with slight panic in his voice.

"We have the boy and even though we know he doesn't have the manna, our Chinese friend doesn't. He had reason enough to kill a priest over the stuff so it's fair to say he'll be hunting down the boy."

Khalil rubbed his hand over his bearded chin and shuffled uncomfortably in his seat.

"We've got you, Khalil, don't worry," Alex said, placing a spread of cold meats, cheese and flat bread on the kitchen counter.

"The guy is an experienced killer, Alex. I mean no disrespect but you're a woman. How are you going to keep us safe?"

"Oh, this wife of mine isn't like any other woman, my friend. She has skills of her own that will send any assailant running. Trust me." Sam tucked into the food, motioning for Khalil to help himself.

"So you're on your honeymoon, on the South coast of Italy, and yet here you are caught in the middle of a murder. You could just let us go to the police and let them straighten it out."

"Did you have a good look at the lad? They'll throw the boy in a cell and he'll go down for murder. He wouldn't stand a chance. Trust me, mate, in our line of work we've seen it all. Things aren't always cut and dried."

"Your line of work. What is that exactly?" Khalil pushed.

"Private antiquity recovery. If we can put it in simple terms, we're the good guys, trained by the professionals to handle exactly these kinds of situations," Sam assured their new associate. "Come on, my friend. I suggest you get some sleep and leave the rest to us. You're in good hands."

. . .

When Khalil and Stavros stepped out on deck the next morning, Alex and Sam were on the flybridge helm. Bari was already a fair distance behind them as the small luxury motor yacht navigated its way through the Adriatic waters in the direction of Stavros' remote Ionian island.

"You look like you slept well considering how anxious you were last night," Alex commented as Khalil took a seat next to her.

"Like a rock, yes. It's easier when you let go and allow God to protect you," Khalil responded.

"Seems our young man also slept well. Any chance he remembered anything else about our Chinese friend?" Sam nudged.

"Nothing that makes any sense," Khalil answered. "He's just heartbroken to have to return home with nothing. How far do we have to go?"

"We should be there by late afternoon," Alex answered while pouring them some orange juice.

"That's if all goes well," Sam added, his voice slightly burdened.

"Why wouldn't it?" Khalil responded.

"One should never be too complacent in these situations, Khalil. We had a suspicious looking drone hover over our boat last night."

"Might have just been some curious tourists. We have a lot of them flying around during the summer," Khalil suggested.

"Probably, except this wasn't any old shop-bought drone. It was unmistakably high tech. Besides, we were too far away from the harbor which would mean we'd have been out of range for any of the commercial ones," Alex commented.

Khalil grew silent and stepped to one side to light a cigarette.

"That stuff will kill you mate," Sam remarked.

"You sound like my wife, but you're right, of course. I've been trying to quit for years."

The hull sliced through the deep blue water, leaving behind white waves under the boat's powerful engines. Alex searched their surroundings through her binoculars, spotting only a commercial ferry in the far distance and a small pod of dolphins rushing through the water. Even after a few hours, when both Khalil and Stavros took to a game of chess on the main deck, she remained on watch next to Sam. When her back stiffened and she jumped to her feet during another routine scouring through her binoculars, Sam realized she had spotted something.

"What is it?"

"Looks like another boat," she answered as she adjusted the strength of the lenses.

"What type of boat?"

"A speedboat and it's heading directly toward us."

"Let's not take any chances. If it's our Chinese friend, it's very likely he's armed with more than just a knife and I'm certain this time he won't be alone. You should get them downstairs and gear up," Sam cautioned, taking the binoculars from her.

Alex leaped down the ladder to the main deck. "Get downstairs and don't come back out until I tell you to," she instructed as she rushed past Khalil and Stavros into the kitchen.

"Why? What's happening?" Khalil asked, encouraging Stavros to do as they were told.

"We might have some company. It's just a precaution but it's best you both stay out of sight. Can you shoot?"

Khalil stared at the Smith and Wesson .38 Special in her hand.

"It's loaded—five bullets in the cylinder. There's no safety. Just aim and shoot, but whatever you do, try not to shoot into the floor."

Alex placed the revolver on top of the counter before retrieving two more guns from the cupboard. She dropped the magazine of her Glock 17 in her hand and checked that it was loaded before doing the same with a second gun, placing them in her waistband, one on either hip. She reached into the cupboard once more, unzipped a black rifle bag and clicked the scope in place. Khalil stood motionless next to her, his eyes pinned on the weapons.

"It's for self-defense only, Khalil. We're not in the business of killing people," she said, placing his hand over the revolver he hadn't yet taken off the counter.

"As long as the two of you stay down here you'll be fine. Only shoot when your life depends on it, okay?"

When Khalil finally locked himself and Stavros into their cabin, Alex rejoined Sam at the helm.

CHAPTER SIX

"Everything okay down there?" Sam said as he handed her the binoculars.

"He's not the shooting type that's for sure."

"Hopefully it won't get to that."

"Don't hold your breath. Whoever they are, they're gaining on us," Alex reported.

She took one of the Glocks and placed it in front of Sam on the dashboard. As the yacht motored its way through the glistening turquoise waters of the Adriatic sea, Alex kept her eyes fixed on the boat that trailed behind them. As they drew nearer, gaining by the minute, she distinguished the figures of three men on board the fast approaching speedboat.

"There are three of them and they're definitely armed. Looks like automatic rifles. How far away are we from Corfu?"

"At least another two hours but it's pointless to try and beat them there. This yacht wasn't made for speeding through choppy water," Sam replied. "I'm already pushing her more than I should."

"Then we have no choice but to fight them when they catch up to us. I'm ready."

Alex crouched against the backrest of the seating on the flybridge and positioned her Remington 783 across the back of the seat. Using her rifle's scope she set her target on the men in the speedboat. All three of them were masked and now in an upright position. Sam had switched the engines to a steady speed on autopilot and took his position next to her. Armed only with his Glock and the binoculars he fixed his sights on the men. They were standing up, their weapons pointed out from their waists toward the yacht.

"Well, what do you know? They're Chinese all right. If I'm not mistaken those are military issued QBZs," Sam commented, focusing his lenses on the weapons.

"Military issued? They're not in uniform. Do you think they're a renegade group? Why would rebels be after something with absolutely zero religious significance to them?" Alex queried.

"Not sure, but we're about to find out."

Sam's words had barely left his lips when a series of bullets flew over their heads and clanked off the metal railings in front of them. With the precision of a trained sniper, Alex fired and hit the shooter in his shoulder, catapulting him overboard as their boat hit a wave behind the yacht. Instantly the remaining two men opened fire, blasting several rounds through the windows on the main deck of the yacht. The driver pushed the speedboat forward alongside the yacht, affording his sidekick the opportunity to jump on board. From behind the safety of the seating inside the flybridge, Alex fired off another bullet into the speedboat's engines. A tendril of black smoke curled from the engine though it still appeared fully operational—not what she had hoped to achieve. Down below, Sam descended on the intruder with an onslaught of punches and managed to seize his weapon, kicking it across the main deck. When the attacker came at him with a knife, Sam moved to the side and locked his arm around the man's neck. Coming to his associate's defense the driver of the boat fired off a series of bullets at Sam who instinctively used his attacker's body as a shield. Bullets ripped into the man's chest before the impact pushed both him and Sam flat onto the deck. A single bullet left Alex's rifle and sliced through the driver's arm causing him to jerk the steering wheel to one side. The boat spun out of control in the wake of the yacht and Alex fired off another bullet into its engines. This time clouds of black smoke wafted into the air moments before it caught fire and exploded.

"Sam!" Alex shouted, while she pulled the yacht's kill switch from the dashboard. Rushing down to the main deck she found Sam lying underneath his attacker's inert body.

"Sam, can you hear me?" Alex shouted and pushed the barely alive attacker off him.

Sam didn't show any sign of life. She moved his head from side to side looking for any bullet wounds then moved her eyes to his torso. His shirt was drenched in blood. Uncertain whether it was the attacker's or Sam's, her fingers ripped through the thin fabric. Much to her relief there were no signs that he had been shot.

"Sam, talk to me," she said sternly. Still he didn't react. "Sam, can you hear me?" She slammed her fists down hard onto his chest. The pounding was enough to bring her husband back from his unconscious state as he drew in a sharp breath.

"You're okay, just breathe," she instructed before turning her attention to the wounded assailant next to her. He was still alive but several bullets had pierced his chest and arms. She pulled the mask off his face and, as expected, recognized the man to be of Chinese descent.

"Who are you?" Alex demanded an answer but the man's glazed-over eyes stared back at her. He was barely alive. Again she pushed him for an answer. "Who are you? Why are you after the manna?" Still he didn't answer. Instead he spat a ball of blood into her face. Alex ignored the act of disrespect, shaking him by the shoulders. "Tell me who you are, you coward!" she shouted.

Still the man didn't respond. A faint sadistic smile came over his face just before he gasped for air, his mouth full of blood, and exhaled his last breath.

"Is he dead?" Sam groaned as he tried to catch his breath.

Alex nodded. "You okay?"

"I will be once I can breathe again. The bugger knocked the wind out of me."

"His body saved your life. That was quick thinking." She

helped Sam to his feet and set him down on the nearby chair. "I should go check on the others."

Alex descended into the hull and found Khalil on the floor halfway up against a cupboard, his shirt drenched with blood.

"No, no, no! What have you done? Sam!" she shouted back for help.

A quick glance over revealed Khalil had been shot in the abdomen but was still alive. She grabbed a dish towel and pushed it down onto the bleeding wound. He was at least lucid and responsive but was losing blood fast.

"Go check on Stavros," Sam said when he staggered down the steps and fell to his knees next to Khalil.

"What have you done, mate? We told you to stay in the cabin," Sam said as he lifted Khalil's back away from the cupboard.

"I tried to help," Khalil groaned with pain. "I thought I could help," he moaned again.

"It's going to be okay. Just relax," Sam answered while his fingers ripped through his bloodied shirt to inspect the wound.

"I can't die," Khalil moaned again.

"You're not dying today, Khalil. Looks like the bullet passed right through you, my friend and, judging by the location of the exit wound, the bullet just missed your kidneys."

Moments later Alex returned having left Stavros in the cabin.

"He's fine, in shock, but fine." She looked at Khalil's drained face where he now lay flat on his back. "How bad is it?"

"Once I stop the bleeding and stitch him up he should be just fine. It's a through and through. Miraculously the bullet missed all his vital organs. I suspect it hit a blood vessel or two so I'm going to have to act fast before he loses more blood. I'd say he's one lucky man."

Alex lifted Sam's medical supplies bag out from the storage compartment under the seating and opened it onto the floor next to him. In typical fashion Sam was fully prepared for any eventuality; his medical background served him well.

"The yacht seems intact; apart from the broken windows and bullet holes everywhere. These guys meant business, that's certain," Alex reported as she hooked the IV bag onto the cupboard's handle above her head.

Sam didn't answer and she watched as his hands skillfully moved over Khalil's bullet wound. At times like this she was convinced he missed being a doctor but he never talked about it and she never asked.

A little over an hour later Sam had managed to stop the bleeding. Khalil was in a stable condition, sedated and recovering in his bed. As to be expected, Stavros was badly traumatized by the series of events that had nearly killed him twice already and Sam thought it best to give him a mild sedative too.

Alex had steered the yacht a safe distance away from where

the speedboat's debris still floated somewhere off the coast of Albania. Apart from the shattered windows and bullet holes in the furniture, she had managed to restore the boat to a semi decent state and gathered most of the bullet casings along the way. Sam eventually found her, standing hands on her hips over the assailant's dead body.

"There's nothing on the man. No identity, no phone, nothing," she said.

Sam squatted down on his haunches and ran his eyes over the body.

"What about tattoos?"

"I've already checked. There's nothing."

He pushed one of the sleeves up anyway. When it didn't reveal any markings he proceeded to do the same with the other one. There was nothing but a cheap gold wristwatch.

"You were right, by the way. They shot with QBZs but I'm very certain these guys weren't in any Chinese law enforcement agency."

"I agree. So unless they managed to somehow buy the weapons on the black market, my guess is they had friends in high places who supplied their weapons. That certainly also accounts for the high-tech nature of last night's drone. It could've locked into our GPS which explains how they managed to find us in the middle of the ocean."

"Well, then let's hope it blew up with the boat," Alex added.

Sam slipped the watch off the dead man's wrist in the hope of finding an inscription but there was none. Alex tilted her head to one side when she noticed the small marking on the inside of his wrist and traced the raised lines on his skin.

"Can you read Chinese?" she joked.

"Last time I checked I couldn't, but Google can. Why?"

"It looks like he was branded."

Alex flicked through the screens on her phone and copied the text to an app. She frowned. "That's odd. It's just a number. Forty-nine. Mean anything to you."

Sam shook his head and rose to his feet. "It's probably nothing."

"Then why was it hidden under his watch?" Alex queried as she took a photo of it with her phone.

Sam shrugged his shoulders. "I have no idea but I know he can't stay here. We're going to have to throw him overboard, Alex... gun and all. We can't leave any traces behind. If they are as connected as I suspect, we'll end up dead or in a Chinese prison and never see daylight again. But one thing is clear. These guys were acting on orders and whoever sent them won't stop until they find the boy. We need to cover our tracks and make sure he's safe. As long as they believe he has the manna they will continue to hunt him down."

"Then we need to find the manna before they find Stavros."

CHAPTER SEVEN

Though still baffled by the man's obscure etching, Alex helped Sam dispose of the body and whatever evidence they'd managed to retrieve on the yacht. They knew the body would eventually wash up somewhere, but they took every precaution for it not to be traced back to them. As dusk fell across the ocean and Khalil and Stavros remained asleep in their cabin, Sam steered the yacht onward to their destination.

Alex was restless as she sat next to Sam in the flybridge. It was late spring and the sun's last orange rays were disappearing beneath the waves of the dark blue ocean. As she continued to stare out over the sea, the cool evening air had her pull a chunky knit throw over her legs and tuck it in under her armpits. In the distance, Corfu's lights danced on the horizon and her thoughts trailed to the teenage boy down below deck whose lot now fell on them. His courage was admirable, she thought, as she made a mental note to enquire about his age when he woke up. To have journeyed the distance he had, all in the hope of a magic fluid gathered from a centuries-old skeleton, took more than courage. It took faith. She tried to recall how it was that she knew the Bible story about the manna, but she couldn't and instead soon found herself pondering over what Khalil had lost, all in the name of his faith.

Her eyes settled on Sam and she suddenly found herself doubting if she ought to have married him. What if she lost him? Had she been a fool to open her heart to him in the first place, just to run the risk of losing him? But then she recalled her father quoting some poet the morning of their wedding; *'It is better to have loved and lost than never to have loved at all.'*

She smiled and let the cool evening breeze blow away her fears. She couldn't imagine a life without Sam.

hen Sam gently kissed her forehead, she realized she must have dozed off.

"We're here, sweetheart," he whispered.

"What time is it?"

"It's late. We should get some rest and I need to check on Khalil."

A sudden chill washed over her body.

"What if they tracked us here?" Alex asked, suddenly wide awake.

"I disconnected the GPS when we dumped the body. Mathraki's main port is on the other side of the island. I thought it best to hide here on the east side until morning. I doubt anyone will find us here, but to be on the safe side you should also remove your phone's SIM."

Alex placed a cup of coffee next to Sam on his nightstand and turned to go back into the kitchen.

"You're up early," he said in a sleepy voice as he sat up to take a sip of the coffee.

"You can blame Stavros for that. The boy's stomach had him rummaging through the kitchen at the crack of dawn."

"Is he okay?" Sam asked.

"Seems so, yes. I think he's relieved to have made it home safely, albeit without the manna."

"Hopefully you're right about his mother just having a bad case of the flu. Judging from the size of this island it's hard to imagine they have any medical care at all. Have you checked on Khalil?" he asked.

"Yup, he's awake. The IV's run out during the night and he's in quite a bit of pain so you might want to hurry it along. Breakfast is almost ready."

Stavros devoured his cheese and tomato omelet before helping himself to another breakfast roll. Alex watched him from where she stood drinking her coffee in the kitchen. His messy ash-brown hair fell gently across his forehead and just about covered his prominent eyebrows and striking green eyes. He looked younger than the fifteen years he claimed to be; a question she'd had Khalil ask him earlier. He was just a child.

A wave of anxiety ripped through Alex's insides when she realized that his trip had taken him away from home for almost two weeks. It would be a travesty if his mother had passed away in his absence. She hurriedly placed her cup on the counter and made her way to where Sam was replacing the dressing on Khalil's wound.

"We need to get a move on, Sam. I'd never forgive myself if anything happened to the boy's mother while he was gone."

"You're right," Sam said and turned back to address Khalil. "There's no infection, my friend. You're one lucky man. You'll be up and at it in no time. Just keep still and let the meds do the work while we get the boy home. We'll be back in no time."

Sam had given him more medication, the strength of which would render him asleep for most of the day, and before long the three of them were on the dinghy making their way to the shore. A small flock of seagulls hit the water with force several yards away from them, ascending just as suddenly with the catch of the day. As they neared the shoreline, Stavros jumped into the water and pulled the dinghy closer to the beach. In front of them the island looked entirely unpopulated and in direct contrast to the bustling shores of Corfu and the other popular Greek islands. Mathraki was eerily tranquil. Alex and Sam allowed Stavros to lead the way across the beach to the foot of a large sand dune topped with wild trees and colorful flora. Having lived there all his life it was evident he knew his way around the small island. He beckoned for them to hurry, ostensibly also experiencing a sense of urgency to get back to his mother. The sand was firm beneath their feet as Alex and Sam followed the boy over the sand dune. Alex briefly looked back. From the top of the dune they had a spectacular view across the ocean. The sun's rays glistened off the blue-green water surrounding the yacht.

"Stop worrying. There's no way they'd find us." Sam offered Alex some assurance.

He was right. Without the GPS there'd be no way anyone could track them. They continued over a few more sand dunes, upsetting a family of pheasants along the way, to where a narrow road divided it from the next set. It was already quite hot as the morning sun beat down on them and they struggled to keep up with the boy's pace.

"Slow down, lad. You're less than half our age," Sam teased, knowing full well the boy didn't understand a word of English.

The road's powdery white sand gradually transformed into off-white gravel and about a quarter of a mile further on the cobalt blue roof of a taverna welcomed them.

"Well, what do you know? There is in fact life on this island," Sam said sarcastically.

The sighting of the taverna propelled Stavros to move even faster and he set off in a fast jog. Sam wiped the sweat from his brow as he and Alex joined in, though still arriving at the taverna well after the boy. Inside the crisp white walls of the taverna, they found Stavros already engrossed in a conversation with a man wearing a white apron over a matching collared shirt. The man's tanned skin sat stark against his white apron and rolled up sleeves. From the entrance, Alex and Sam watched as the man's jaw tightened before his strong arms embraced Stavros. A tall, skinny, apron-wearing brunette ran toward them. Instantly her slender arms folded around the boy who desperately clung onto the older man and moments later two more women were sobbing by their side.

Alex stood in silence as they watched the tragic scene play out in front of them. It was obvious the boy's mother hadn't survived. They were too late. Alex's insides tightened up as her mind flashed back to the day she'd received the news of her own mother's death. Stavros would never see his mother again. Anger surged through her veins. She had failed Stavros. Miserably. Sam could've saved his mother, if only they'd got there sooner.

Her raging thoughts were interrupted when the older man finally walked up to them.

"Thank you for bringing our boy home," he said in a deep voice, his English tainted with a strong Greek accent. He shook Sam's hand and pulled Alex into a grateful embrace.

"Did she... did his mother...?" Alex couldn't finish her question.

"She was a very brave woman," the man announced. "It was better Stavros wasn't here to see her die. She had a lot of pain. Come, come, sit." The man pulled them toward a small table and yelled an instruction at one of the women who promptly arrived with a jug of lemon squash and three glasses. His authority gave away that the taverna belonged to him.

"I'm Doudous," he introduced himself.

Alex and Sam reciprocated.

"What's going to happen to Stavros?" Alex asked.

"Stavros is a strong boy; like his mother. He is like my very own son. I promised her that I will take care of him. We grew up together, here on Mathraki. She was like my sister, family. That's my wife and my two daughters." He pointed to the three women who compassionately sat with Stavros. "He has many people who love him." Doudous dried his eyes with his apron and poured them each a glass of squash.

"Stavros said you helped him. What do you need? I have fresh fish that came in from the boat this morning and my wife is making *souvlaki*. Whatever you need, I'll give you."

Doudous bellowed some Greek words across the restaurant floor.

"We're fine, thank you. I'm sorry we couldn't get here in time to save his mother. Sam's a doctor, well he used to be one, and we had hoped he could have helped her," Alex declared.

"It was her time. No one could have saved her. The cancer was too strong. Stavros had the silly idea in his head that the Saint Nicholas manna would save her. It's all a fairytale, we know that, but I had to at least let the boy try. He would've never forgiven himself if he didn't do something to help his mother."

"So you don't believe the fluid has the power to heal people?" Sam asked.

"Come on, Sam. You're a doctor, you tell me. They are just bones sweating in a closed coffin. The Italians stole the remains from the Turkish and every year they make bags full of money from the tourists, cheating people into thinking it has some supernatural power. Yes, the man was a saint and he did great things for the Turkish and Greek people, but he's been dead for hundreds of years. It's not possible."

Alex looked at Stavros where the women had now put him to work as a means of distracting him. He sat with a bowl of fresh olives on his lap, picking the leaves and stems off before dropping them into a wooden vat on the floor next to him.

"Someone out there disagrees with you, Doudous. They killed the priest and then tried to kill Stavros. There has to be more to it than mere fables," Alex said.

"What do you mean someone tried to kill my boy?"

"Exactly that. The priest somehow ended up dead and the murderer thought Stavros had taken the manna. They've been after us ever since we left Bari."

Doudous rose, placing his big hands on the table and leaned in, the veins bulging in his hairy arms. "You need to leave. If they followed you, we are all in danger."

Sam straightened up and Alex did the same. "No one

followed us, Doudous, I assure you. We hid our boat on the east side of the island. You're safe."

Doudous pulled the linen cloth from his shoulder and wiped the table before flinging it back over his shoulder and clearing the glasses.

"I will not survive if anything happens to Stavros or my daughters. You have to understand that I am all he has and I have to protect him. God speed."

CHAPTER EIGHT

They knew the topic wasn't up for further discussion when Doudous turned without saying another word and took up his place behind the bar next to the kitchen. He had made his position very clear and neither Sam nor Alex could blame him for it. They'd have done the same in his situation. Stavros looked up from the bowl of olives in his lap. His once piercing green eyes had been replaced with a dull green tinge resemblant of the very olives he held in his hands. The corners of his mouth lifted in the faintest of smiles for the briefest of moments. He lifted his arm and gently waved a farewell at them before he continued plucking the leaves from the olives in his lap. There was nothing more Alex or Sam could do or say to the boy. His life had changed and would never be the same again. But, as Alex and Sam quietly walked along the white dirt road and back over the overgrown sand dunes, they each silently resolved to hunt down the priest's murderer and establish the truth about the saintly fluid Stavros had risked everything for, believing that it had enough power to heal his mother and save the world. Some might call it revenge, but they called it restitution.

And in the depths of her heart, hidden from her new husband, Alex made her own silent vow. She had lived through the pain of losing a mother and she'd witnessed the very same suffering in Stavros' eyes. It would be a pain she would never bring upon or bear witness to again.

T heir moods remained somber as they each absorbed the drastic turn of events. Allowing each other time to digest was a coping mechanism they had learned over the many years of working together. And when they eventually reached the dinghy and found their way back to their yacht through the cool blue waters surrounding the Ionian island, they spoke again for the first time since leaving the taverna.

"I'm going to check on Khalil and take a swim to clear my head. Care to join me?" Sam invited.

"Sounds like a great idea, yes. Are you hungry? I can make you a sandwich," Alex replied.

"We'll get the guy and the manna, Alex. I promise you. For the boy's sake." Sam promised as he took his wife in his arms.

"I'm going to hold you to that." She smiled and followed him below deck where she got started in the kitchen.

She had barely taken the bread from the basket when Sam darted from the cabin into the bathroom and back out again.

"What's wrong?" Alex said startled.

"He's gone," Sam answered as he sped past her onto the deck.

"What do you mean he's gone? The man's recovering from a gunshot wound. There's no way he could get up and move around. We're in the middle of the ocean," she added doubling up on his search.

"Khalil!" Sam shouted as he searched the yacht before eventually climbing up to the flybridge.

Horror ripped through Sam's body when his eyes settled on the back of Khalil's shoulders. Sitting in the captain's seat, Khalil wasn't moving. As Sam spun the chair around his stomach settled in his feet. Khalil's head was slumped forward onto his chest. Blood had run from his nose and the corners of his mouth and dried onto his skin and beard. His left eye was dark red and barely visible under the swollen skin around it. In his lap his hands were bound at his wrists with a translucent cable tie that had already ripped into his flesh. Across his abdomen fresh blood from the gunshot wound had seeped through his dressings and his shirt.

"Khalil!" Sam called, repeating it twice while his fingers checked for a pulse. It was weak but he was still alive. Barely. Sam continued calling out to him, silently praying he'd wake up. A slight frown appeared just above Khalil's thick brows.

"There you are. Hang in there, my friend. You're going to be fine." Sam's hands rummaged through the cupboard below the dashboard and found the small pliers.

"Who did this to you?" He asked a rhetorical question as he snipped through the cable ties.

The muffled reply he received told him Khalil was in no position to speak. Instinctively his eyes settled on Khalil's mouth. There was too much blood. Fear tugged at the pit of his stomach when the thought crossed his mind that they might have done something far worse. He braced himself and gently parted Khalil's lips and jaw and found something entirely different.

"Spit it out, mate," he urged Khalil who was barely conscious but groaned under the strain of Sam's fingers on his jaw.

"What is it?" Alex spoke behind him, surprised that Sam hadn't heard her come up behind him.

Sam didn't answer as he pulled out the crumpled ball of paper from Khalil's broken jaw and dropped it on the floor next to them. Alex, without conscious thought, stooped to pick it up, closing her hand over the paper before shoving it inside the pocket of her pants. The sun was relentless and time was crucial. Getting Khalil out of the heat was priority. So when they eventually lay him down in his bed, Sam sprang to work on his injuries. The gunshot wound had opened up and required new stitches and redressing. Sam cleaned up the fresh wounds and skillfully treated what he could. They had broken his jaw and several ribs, the jaw requiring more than he was capable of offering outside of a hospital. It took the best part of an hour for the painkillers to work and Khalil's heartrate to return to a semi stable state and when Sam finally left Khalil's side, he found Alex sitting in the small saloon area on the deck.

"How is he?" she asked.

"We're going to need to get him to a hospital, Alex. There's only so much I can do here. He needs proper medical equipment and surgery to repair his jaw. It's impossible to see just how bad the damage is without scans."

Alex didn't have the words to reply. She took the blood-stained piece of paper Sam had pulled from Khalil's mouth and flattened it out on the small wooden table in front of her. She sat back and allowed Sam to take it in before she spoke.

"We might not be able to do that, Sam."

Sam stared at the note he now had in his hand. The words punched him in his stomach as he struggled to make sense of it all. His eyes conveyed his inner turmoil while Alex waited for him to respond.

"Who are these people? How did they even find us?" His voice was saturated with anger as he now stood gazing out into the open sea behind them, struggling to control his temper.

"I checked. The GPS is still disconnected and both our phones' SIM cards were removed. Then I found this." Alex put the black iPhone on the table. "It's the dead guy's. We somehow missed it when we cleaned up the yacht. It must have dropped out of his pocket or something. That's how they found us."

Sam crossed the deck in three strides. His eyes searched the water around them. When his search delivered nothing he looked up into the sky.

"They're not watching, Sam. They've left. They're forcing us to comply with their demands. We don't have a choice. We're going to have to do as they instructed."

Sam wiped his forehead and took a seat opposite Alex. He picked up the note and read it again.

Find the fluid or we kill his wife and daughters
Go to Bari and wait for further instructions
No police

"T hey're good, yes," Alex spoke Sam's thoughts. "This note tells us they know exactly who each of us is. They've done their homework."

"He doesn't deserve this. He's a good man," Sam said, still fighting the anger his body threatened to expel.

"I know, Sam, and it's all my fault. I should've never insisted we go inside that church. It was selfish of me. None of this would have happened had it not been for my curiosity."

"I disagree. Stavros would have been killed or locked up for a murder he didn't commit if we weren't there. Not to mention he wouldn't have been able to get back here."

Unable to sit through his thoughts Sam rose to his feet and took up stance at the railing.

"Khalil is in no position to schlep with us. He needs to be in a hospital. We'll have to take him in."

"They'll be forced to report it to the police, Sam. That's a certain death sentence on Khalil's family, and us for that matter. We can't," Alex argued.

"He'll die without proper care, Alex. The guy's ribs are broken and if any of them puncture his lung it's over. Never mind his broken jaw! He needs X-rays and MRIs, surgery, more meds, the list goes on."

"What about Yusuf? He might know of a private clinic," Alex suggested.

"And drag another one of his family members into this? Not a good idea."

"Well we're out of options and fast running out of time. It's a good ten hours back to Bari. We're going to have to do something and fast."

Sam rubbed the stubble on his clenched jaw as he paced the breadth of the deck.

"I might know someone," he finally said, in a voice that divulged uncertainty.

"Who?"

"He worked with my father back in the day and if memory serves me right , he's now living out his retirement in Lake Como."

"Great, let's go," Alex urged as she started making her way to the flybridge, pausing when Sam remained seated.

"We need to go, Sam."

"They're still friends," Sam declared as he nervously rubbed his hands up and down his thighs.

"Yes, that's a good thing, right?"

Sam stopped his pacing and again took up his place next to the railing.

"Sam, what's going on?" Alex said with confusion in her voice.

"They're friends, Alex. That's the problem. My father thinks I'm still practicing medicine at King Edward," Sam blurted out.

Alex gasped. "You never told your parents you left medicine and shifted careers?"

He nodded. "I know it's ridiculous, but it would kill my father if he knew his only son broke the Quinn fourth generation medical lineage. And that for something as arbitrary as archaeology. He'd never live it down."

"So all these years you've kept it secret?"

"Only to protect him. I told my mother a few years back."

Alex walked over and placed her hands on the railing next to him.

"Maybe he won't say anything. I mean, how often would they still speak to each other? We either chance it or drop Khalil at a hospital ourselves and disappear before anyone asks us anything. His jaw is broken so he won't be able to talk for a while. It might give us enough time to find the manna and put this entire ordeal behind us. We have about ten hours to decide so let's get the show on the road. It'll be fine, promise."

CHAPTER NINE

Their yacht slowly motored into the Bari port in the early hours of the morning. Absolute tranquility replaced the manic chaos of the events that had surrounded their departure, bringing them some relief considering what still lay ahead. Sam and Alex had both had a restless night having had to take turns between steering the yacht and tending to Khalil, whose condition had taken a turn for the worse. When Sam fastened the yacht to their mooring and descended below deck to fetch Khalil, Alex asked what she hoped he'd decided by now.

"How do you want to handle this then? Call your father's friend or shall we risk taking him into hospital ourselves."

Sam had already removed the intravenous drip from Khalil's arm and lifted him to his feet, careful not to inflict more injury to his broken ribs.

"See if you can find a taxi parked nearby. We're taking him to the hospital," he replied without explaining his decision any further.

Alex complied and headed down the short pier towards where several taxis were parked along the coastal road. The taxi driver, who had been asleep, eagerly took the job when she promised him almost five times the normal rate to take their friend to the hospital, so much so that he illegally drove his taxi down onto the pier to get as close as possible to where Sam waited with Khalil.

"Want to talk about it?" Alex nudged after Khalil had left with the taxi driver who had received a bonus payment from Sam for telling the hospital he'd picked Khalil up off the side of the road.

"I'd rather tell my father to his face," Sam said. "Besides, Khalil was in no condition for us to gamble with time or to call for special favors. It would have taken at least a day for anyone to travel here. It had to be done."

They walked in silence back to the yacht.

"Now what?" Sam said as they got on board.

"Now we wait," Alex said. "The note said to wait for further instructions."

They each slept with one eye open until the sun's rays poured through their small cabin window. Sam had placed a call to the hospital who confirmed a man had been brought in and was in stable condition. He hung up when they asked for his name.

"Have you managed to find anything on the Chinese guy's phone?" Sam asked when he'd poured himself another cup of coffee and sat next to Alex where she'd been fiddling with the iPhone.

"It's all in Chinese. I've been trying to find the language setting but it's proven to be more challenging than I anticipated."

"I can't sit around like this and do nothing. I say we go to the basilica and see if we can find out from one of the priests if the manna was in fact stolen. For all we know it's there and we can move on," Sam said, his fingers tapping anxiously against the white mug in his hand.

"You're right. It's not going to get us any closer to finding the fluid by just sitting here waiting for them to make contact. IF they make contact. Khalil is in safe hands for now, and as long as he can't speak, the police can't open a case and his family will be safe."

W hen they arrived at the Basilica di San Nicola, the crime scene tape had been removed and the large hand-carved wooden door of the main entrance stood wide open. To the unaware, it appeared as if nothing had ever happened—even the crimson stain on the doorsteps had been cleaned away. Once inside, the warm glow of a multitude of prayer candles flickered against the limestone walls, and the angelic voices of ten or so altar boys, who stood in an organized huddle in the back of the church, filled every corner of the holy space. A few tourists roamed between the transepts in awe of the spectacular nave and decorative arches above them; mesmerized by the gold embellishments around the religious paintings on the ceiling. The ambience was entirely different from their secret and almost fatal rendezvous only a few days before, and Alex and Sam couldn't help being hypnotized by its beauty. As they made their way to the front of the church, several devotees were seated in the dark wood pews; some just blankly staring at the huge amber stained-glass cross in the arched window behind the altar, and others prayerfully running their fingers through the beads in their rosaries on their laps. Again, in total contrast to their last visit, the black wrought-iron cage was no longer surrounding the altar over the crypt that now stood in spectacular glory in front of the church. Illuminated by the warm glow of overhanging lights the detail was astounding. It was as if a lace tablecloth, carved entirely from marble and limestone, was draped over the crypt while a multitude of small pillars held up an equally impressive canopy above it. Alex found herself taking a seat, against her will, in the front pew. Sam sat down next to her.

"I'm weak at the knees too," Sam whispered. "It's quite something, isn't it?"

Alex nodded. "I've never experienced anything like it."

She turned back and glimpsed the figure of a priest stepping into the confession box in the back of the church.

"We should get on with it," she whispered as she jumped to her feet and walked toward the ornate wooden stall.

"You're not going in there, are you?" Sam stopped her when she was about to open the confessional door.

"Do you have a better idea? There's a priest inside and from what I've seen in the movies he can't see your face. It can't be more in our favor."

"All right then," Sam smiled knowing she had never set foot inside a confessional before, "I do see your point. I'll go around to the bell tower in search of the caretaker and meet you back here."

Alex didn't hesitate as she opened the narrow wooden door and settled on the velvet covered burgundy stool. The dark space made her feel somewhat claustrophobic and reminded her of a closet. The panel next to her head slid open causing her to push her back further against the panel behind her. No one spoke so she cleared her throat and called out a greeting. "Hello?"

The priest cleared his throat.

"Oh yes, of course," she stumbled over her words as she recalled a scene from a film she watched some time ago. "Bless me, Father, for I have sinned, although technically speaking I didn't sin. It was purely self-defense. Anyway, I just need some information from you," she blurted out.

It sounded like the priest almost choked before he cleared his throat once more and replied in a calmer than expected voice.

"How did you not sin? Everyone sins."

"I'm sure you're right, but in this case, I merely shot back to protect the boy and Khalil. It was kill or be killed. If we hadn't defended ourselves we'd all be dead."

Alex sensed the clergyman's face in the panel as he tried to take a look at her. She pulled her head back flush with the panel between them.

"And, did you?" he asked.

"Did I what?"

"Kill someone."

Alex suddenly felt uncomfortable. The thought of leaving crossed her mind. It wasn't something she enjoyed doing or ever thought would be a normality in her life. But killing was what was expected when situations called for it.

"I need to ask you about the manna." She ignored the priest's question.

"I would strongly urge you to repent of your sins," the priest said calmly.

"Look, I'm not Catholic so I'm not even sure how all this works, but what I do know is that the manna is at threat of being stolen and people were killed over it. I'm not the enemy. I'm here to help." It was her turn to look through the slatted screen. Her eyes met those of the priest who, even though he was caught off guard, didn't turn away.

"Please follow me," he whispered.

Alex heard his hand on the door handle and hurried out. As promised, Sam was already waiting for her.

"What's happening?" he whispered as he scrambled to his feet and stepped into pace alongside her.

"I'm not sure. He said to follow him."

The priest was several strides ahead of them and somewhat in a hurry. As Alex and Sam pushed to keep up with him, he led them out through the main entrance and in through another smaller wooden door at the front of the building. Once inside, the space almost immediately narrowed into a long corridor with several more rooms leading off on each side. The doors were all shut, apart from one about halfway down which he ushered them through. He closed the door behind them as they stepped inside the small office. In front of the arched window stood a dark wood desk that faced the door behind them. He pointed them to the two red velvet chairs directly in front of the desk before moving behind a third chair that stood behind his desk. He didn't sit and instead paused with his hands on the backrest. With the glowing sunlight pouring in through the window behind him, the middle-aged priest almost looked saintly in its glow. His skin was the color of ivory and his eyes were a warm hazel color accentuated by his matching thick, neatly-trimmed hair.

"Who are you?" he asked, this time with his tone more urgent than the one he'd used within the confessional.

"I'm Alex and this is Sam."

Alex couldn't help but wonder if he was the same man she had just spoken to in the confession box.

"No, I meant who sent you and why are you asking about the manna?"

Again his voice was in direct contrast to the calm, saintly one from before. As if he sensed her question he de-robed, throwing the cassock over the back of his chair before pulling his white collar from the neck of his black shirt and dropping it on the desk before them. He rolled his sleeves up as if he meant business and then sat down at his desk.

"We haven't been sent by anyone," Sam answered, "and as for the manna, we didn't know anything about it until a few days ago."

With his hands clenched on top of his desk, he spoke even more firmly.

"Why are you here?"

"Look, Father, we're not here to cause trouble. Quite the contrary. We're here to help. We recover stolen artifacts for a living," Alex said.

"You said you had killed people," the priest continued.

"Not deliberately. It's often necessary in our line of work when the lines get too blurry. We were here the day your fellow clergyman was murdered; we assume because of the manna. Now our friend's life is at stake as well as ours. It's a simple case of being in the wrong place at the wrong time. Someone is after the manna and they're blackmailing us into finding it," Alex confessed, annoyed with herself over the fact that she somehow felt compelled to divulge everything to the priest even though it went against her better judgment. And that when she didn't even know his name.

The priest rose and, with his hands behind his back, stared out of the window.

"Can we trust you?" he asked without turning.

A quick glance at Sam confirmed he was as surprised as she was at the priest's unexpected question.

"You can trust us," Sam answered, integrity cemented in each word.

"Wait here," the priest instructed before he left the room.

Alone in the private office, Alex turned to Sam.

"Something tells me we haven't even scratched the surface, Sam. There's a whole lot more going on here than either of us could even begin to imagine. Mark my words."

CHAPTER TEN

S am wasn't given an opportunity to agree with her since the door behind them swung open and two more priests walked into the room.

"This is Father Guido and Father Enzo. I'm Father Roberto, you can call me Father Rob.

Alex followed the trio of Italian clergy with her eyes to where they stood with Father Rob in the center. It was an odd picture, the three of them. Father Guido, tall and slender, Father Enzo, short and stocky, and Father Rob the handsome one whom she recognized as the priest who'd consoled the altar boy the day of the murder.

"It was Father Francesco who was murdered a few days ago," Father Rob started. "We've tried going to the police but we suspect they have been bribed to look the other way. If we can trust you as you say we can, we'd like to take you up on your offer to help."

It took everything for Alex to keep her jaw from dropping to her chest.

"What's going on here, Father?" Sam asked.

Father Rob took his seat behind the desk.

"Our lives are at stake too. Over the past month we've each been receiving death threats. At first we didn't know about each other's threats, but when Father Francesco ended up dead, it all came out," he divulged.

"It seems Father Francesco had been getting these threats well before any of us," Father Guido added.

"How are you receiving the threats?" Alex asked.

"In the beginning it came through one or two phone calls," said Father Enzo.

"Naturally we ignored them. It's not the first time people have attempted to get their hands on a vial of the manna acting out of sheer desperation for an infirm loved one," Father Guido cut in.

"Yes, but then the phone calls stopped and the threats became more serious." It was the familiar stern voice of Father Rob who continued; he appeared to be leading the trio.

"Why, what happened?" Sam enquired.

"That's the horrific part. We each found one of our younger church members, left for dead on our doorsteps at our homes. They were badly beaten. What made it especially cruel was that their jaws were broken and they each had a note stuffed inside their mouths," Father Rob continued.

"Do you still have the notes?" Sam asked.

"No. We foolishly gave them to the police thinking they were going to act on it. They've been giving us the runaround since then," Father Guido said, clearly fighting to control his composure. He was the feisty one, Alex realized.

Alex took the piece of paper from her pocket and flattened it out on the desk in front of the three clergymen. "Did they look like this?"

After a quick glance Father Guido started pacing the room, one hand on his hip and the other rubbing the back of his head. Father Enzo, the timid cautious one, Alex concluded, crossed his arms and nervously looked to Father Rob for guidance.

"Yes. Exactly like that," Father Rob confirmed. "Different messages, but they looked identical."

"Do you have any idea who might be sending these threats?" Sam asked.

The three priests exchanged anxious glances, silently communicating between themselves. A brief nod from each concluded they had agreed on something.

"We just need to be clear that we don't have any proof whatsoever," Father Enzo jumped ahead before Father Guido abruptly added, "But it can only be them. They've been at our throats about it for centuries."

Alex and Sam looked to Father Rob for clarification.

"We suspect it might be Turkey." His voice trailed off at the end of his sentence.

"Turkey, as in the Turkish government?" Alex queried.

"In a manner of speaking yes, but we're actually referring to the church."

"The Roman Catholic church, in Turkey," Alex repeated, even more surprised than the first time he'd said it.

None of them answered. Instead, Father Guido stood like a gorilla with his fists on the desk while Father Enzo placed his fingers over his mouth and Father Rob calmly sat with his hands folded on the desk.

This time Alex paced the room. "Do you realize how insane that sounds? You're accusing a Christian organization of murdering one of their own. Not to mention sending death threats and bribing the police. That's ridiculous!"

"We know, but who else? Ever since the sailors stole the remains of Saint Nicholas, the Turks have been relentless in their efforts to get them back," Father Guido explained.

"Look, we don't like it any more than you do, and yes, it sounds ridiculous considering it's been going on for ages, but it's true." Father Enzo finally spoke.

"It might make more sense to us if you tell us how and when this happened," Sam said.

Father Rob sat back in his chair, paused to gather his words, then told the story.

"It was 1087, Bari was conquered by the Normans and plunged into depression. Once a Byzantine regional capital, it slowly slipped into decay and was at threat of anonymity from the world. The city needed saving from being plunged into total economic ruin. At the time, Christianity was in popular demand and every town was scrabbling for saintly relics. The bigger the saint, the greater the prestige and the more pilgrims would be attracted to the town. Saint Nicholas was the epitome of all saints since his post-death reputation had turned into a cult that swept across Europe. Everyone wanted him, especially Venice, but Bari beat them to it. Seventy sailors embarked on an intrepid two-thousand-mile journey to the city of Myra—now known as Demre, a city in ancient Lycia on the south coast of Turkey. They arrived in three ships in the middle of the night and conned their way into the tomb, smashed it open, and fled with the bones in hand back to their ships. Chased by a mob of Saracens they triumphantly escaped and made it back here with all but a few fragments of Saint Nicholas' skeleton. He's been under lock and key here ever since. Bari would be nothing but a dot on the map if it weren't for the leaking manna."

"So it is all fake. A marketing tactic to make money off people who believe they will be healed by the manna." Alex's voice was thick with disgust as she spoke.

The priests exchanged another silent communication.

"I'm afraid not, Alex. It's a miraculous thing. The fluid has indeed healed many. The blind place the liquid on their eyes and days after they're able to see, the deaf can hear, limbs have grown back, cancer healed, the list goes on," Father Guido declared.

"And that brings us to the question. Where is the manna now?" It was Sam who asked. As a man of science he found it a difficult concept to wrap his head around, but he held back his opinion.

"No one knows. Usually it is tapped during the ceremony, but with what happened to Father Francesco, we never had the ceremony and so the liquid was never extracted, at least not by one of us. We tried to extract it while the police were chasing after the murderer, but the crypt had already been emptied. We suspect the murderer must have found some way of sneaking in before he managed to evade the police."

"He doesn't have it," Sam declared.

"How do you know? Do you know who murdered Father Francesco?" Father Guido was quick to respond, his fists in gorilla-like fashion on the table again.

"No, but we know who the police chased that day. He was innocent; nothing but a young lad desperate to help his dying mother, that's all. He was hiding when he heard the screams and was spotted by the altar boy when he tried to get away." Sam defended Stavros in his absence.

"We need to find out what the police know," Alex suggested.

"It won't help. They're in on it," Father Guido turned and stared out the window.

"That might be, but our only lead now is the notes. We need to see at least one other note to compare ours with; see if there's anything that might point us in the right direction. You need to get your notes back."

"That's impossible! They probably destroyed them already," Father Guido spoke.

"Wait, you said you gave the police *your* notes. What about Father Francesco? If we're to assume he received the same threats as the rest of us, perhaps he kept a note from his victim," Alex thought out loud.

Without a word Father Enzo's short, plump body wobbled out of the office and returned moments later with a Bible which he placed on the desk in front of them. His fat fingers hurriedly flipped through the Bible, allowing a stack of pages through his thumb one batch at a time. When the pages in one of the batches parted naturally he joyfully exclaimed. "I knew it! Here it is."

He stood back and allowed the rest of the small party to take it in.

"You had it all this time, Enzo, and you never said a word," Father Guido said in his now familiar passive aggressive voice.

"I didn't. It's Francesco's Bible. I just recalled him once sharing how he often kept important notes in his Bible. It was lying next to him the day he was killed, so I picked it up and kept it in my office."

Sam took the piece of paper from the Bible and spread it out on the table. "It's the same. 'Give us the manna or you die'," Sam read it out.

Alex placed it next to Khalil's note. "The writing is the same; same ink, same paper."

"But that's it. We're no better off than we were ten minutes ago," Father Guido said with frustration.

"Perhaps not," Alex said. "We need you to do us a favor. The man they beat up is lying in hospital. We can't be seen with him for fear of his family's lives and we've not been able to speak to him since the attack. We need you to get Sam in to see him; disguised as a priest, to find out if Khalil remembers anything. The police would have been informed but his jaw was also broken, so I doubt they would've gotten far."

The clergymen's discomfort was obvious.

"Look, I know it's a lot to ask and we mean no disrespect against the church, but it's the only way in."

Father Guido snickered, "Oh, it's not using the robe that offends us, it's the fact that he's a Turk and that you expect he would tell us anything."

Alex was taken aback realizing they derived Khalil's lineage from her giving them his name.

"He's a Turk but he's also a Christian who was ostracized for it. He lost his wife and two daughters as a result of his faith. He's a good man and didn't deserve to be dragged into this," Sam said sternly.

Father Guido started to protest but Father Rob held up his hand and cut him short.

"No, Guido. It's time this ends. Too many have suffered at the hands of this senseless feud. If it will help us find Francesco's murderer and discover who's behind all of this, we should do it. Besides, let's not forget the fact that the manna is out there somewhere and any of us could be next if we don't find it."

He turned to Sam. "Come with me."

CHAPTER ELEVEN

Dressed as a Catholic priest, Sam entered the San Paulo general hospital with Father Rob at his side. It didn't take much to get Khalil's ward number from the hospital receptionist. As luck would have it, in her mid-fifties, Luciana was one of the regular devotees and knew Father Rob well, and as such, was all too keen to divulge that Khalil had had some odd-looking visitors the day before. Father Rob switched their conversation to English, for Sam's sake, and repeated the information.

"What do you mean 'odd looking'?" Sam queried.

She didn't answer at first until Father Rob assured her Sam was there to temporarily take on a few of Father Francesco's duties.

"They were just odd. As far as I could tell they were Asian. We don't often get Asian people visiting patients. Naturally we didn't let them through since the police hadn't even inter-rogated the patient. It is after all hospital policy and I wasn't going to break it no matter how intimidating they were," she said, as if she felt the need to let the priest know she wasn't planning on breaking any rules for him either.

"How many were there?" Sam asked again.

"Two, but there were more waiting in their car over there." She pointed to where they had parked outside the main entrance of the hospital.

After Father Rob thanked her, he and Sam found a badly bruised Khalil in his bed.

"How are you my friend?" Sam greeted as Khalil's eyes opened to receive them. Under his swollen and wired jaw he could tell Khalil was amused at his robed disguise.

"Yes, yes, desperate times. You okay, mate?" Sam flipped his hospital file open but popped it back into its place since he couldn't understand the Italian notes and instead moved to read the label on the drip. "Think you can get up?" Sam continued.

"What? No, that wasn't what was agreed," Father Rob protested as Sam's plan dawned on him.

"Father, those guys came back to finish the job. Khalil knows something and it's quite obvious they don't want him to share it. If we leave him in here he's as good as dead.

"We can't just take him," the priest continued.

"Why not? He's not under suspicion or arrest for anything, simply recovering from being beaten to a pulp." Sam moved the wheelchair from the other end of the room and helped Khalil in, unclipping the IV bag and placing it in his lap.

Khalil let out a low murmur under his clenched jaw and pointed his splinted arm to the small locker next to the bed.

"Oh yes, of course." Sam took his clothing from the locker and stuffed it in an empty medical waste bag.

"I'll distract Luciana, you get him to the car," Father Rob said under his breath, surprising Sam with his sudden change of heart. And distract her he did; by means of inviting her to pray with him.

As a result, their kidnapping went down without a glitch.

"You didn't think we'd leave you here, did you?" Sam joked with Khalil as they drove away from the hospital.

"Now what?" Father Rob asked when his red Fiat Punto turned the corner.

"We get him someplace safe and find out why those thugs came back for him."

They were almost at the church when Father Rob spotted the pale gray Alfa Romeo in his rearview mirror. Deciding to divert at the last minute, he turned away from the church.

"Where are you going?" Sam asked

"I think we're being followed."

Sam spotted the silver-gray car turning the corner behind them. "The banged-up Alfa. I see it. Turn right here," Sam told the priest who did as he was told. With their eyes on the mirrors they watched the car turn in behind them.

"Khalil, it's best you lie down in the seat, mate. Father, can you shake them?"

"I think so. I grew up in these streets."

From beneath his religious attire, Sam took out his gun and swiftly ran through the prep sequence.

"Is that really necessary?" Father Rob objected.

Sam didn't have to answer him. The series of gunshots hitting the Fiat's trunk did so on his behalf. The priest swerved in response to the unexpected violent act but managed to regain control of his car.

"Try to stay calm, Father. Now would be a great time to put your memory to the test and get us out of here."

Father Rob dropped a gear and pushed his foot down on the gas. More bullets hit the back of the car, shattering the rear window. Sam aimed and fired a shot at the Alfa's wheel but missed when Father Rob had to swerve to avoid an oncoming car.

"Someone's going to get killed like this!" he shouted before veering the car off the shoulder and onto an arterial road.

The Alfa was gaining on them. "You're going to have to try harder, Father. They're fast decreasing the distance between us," Sam declared as a bullet whistled through the narrow space between them and shattered the front windscreen. A knee-jerk reaction had the priest almost hitting a lamp post before he managed to straighten the wheels again.

Sirens shrieked through the air as the police now trailed behind the two cars.

"I knew this was a bad idea!" Father Rob yelled as he took another turn around a large traffic circle. "Maybe we should just pull over and explain everything to the police."

More bullets hit the Fiat's body. Civilian vehicles abruptly came to a halt behind them, causing a traffic jam which the Alfa easily circumvented.

"Why aren't the police stopping them?" the priest queried as he watched the two police vehicles deliberately slowing down behind the Alfa.

"I hate to say this, but it seems you were right. They're in on it. Hold still," Sam directed as he leaned the upper half of his body out the window and took aim at the Alfa's right wheel. He fired off a shot and hit his target. The Alfa swerved before it skidded sideways, flipped and rolled multiple times across the road until it smashed into the concrete column of a bridge. Sam watched as three Asian men crawled out of the car.

"You can relax, Father. No one's dead," Sam reported, observing the priest's drained expression.

. . .

hen they arrived back at the basilica, Sam took Khalil inside while Father Rob parked his car a block away.

"What took you so long?" Alex asked when she closed the office door behind them.

"We ran into some trouble," Sam said in response to the stunned faces of Fathers Guido and Enzo as he sat Khalil down on the worn burgundy couch in the office.

"Where's Father Rob?" Father Enzo asked with concern, "and who's this?" Father Guido added.

"Parking his car, and this is Khalil; their latest assault victim, and now their new target."

"What do you mean 'you ran into trouble'?" Alex asked as she moved a hat stand next to Khalil onto which Sam hooked the IV bag.

"They tried to finish the job with Khalil. I guess they feel the need to clean up any loose ends; perhaps thinking that he knows something that could expose them."

Khalil moaned in an attempt to speak but only his lips moved.

"Next thing we knew they were shooting at us," Sam added just as Father Rob burst into the office and leaned his body against the closed door behind him. "You can't stay here. It's the house of God! I won't tolerate you bringing violence into a holy place," he griped, his complexion still a pale gray.

Khalil moaned again.

"I agree," Father Guido added. "This is getting out of control! Your friend here needs to be in a hospital, not here. You say he's a target. That means they won't hesitate to come back for him. We have mass tonight. You have to get him out of here." Father Guido was in his usual stance over the desk.

"Now hold on, Guido. We did ask them to help us. Let's not forget we're all at risk of ending up like Francesco if we don't find the manna and give it to them." It was Father Enzo who spoke, revealing he had more of a backbone than originally thought.

Father Guido moved to the window and a few moments of silence filled the room.

"We understand the predicament we're all in, but Father Guido is correct. We have dozens of devotees coming to mass tonight. It will be grossly negligent of us. You can't stay here," Father Rob agreed.

"You can go to Father Francesco's apartment. They won't suspect you'd be there," the suddenly brazen Father Guido suggested.

Father Rob who still hadn't moved away from the door, agreed. "You're right. I believe if he'd been alive he would have wanted to help in some way. Who knows, we might find another note amongst his things. I'll fetch the car."

And with that he promptly turned and made his way back to his red Fiat.

. . .

hen Father Rob opened the door to Father Francesco's apartment and let Alex, Sam and Khalil in, the apartment had been ransacked.

"Great, so they've been here already," Alex commented, clearing away the mess on the small bed that stood by the window in the studio apartment.

"How is that great?" Father Rob questioned.

"Well, it means that they won't likely be back since they've already searched the place. My guess is they were hoping to find the manna here."

Khalil moaned again.

"Okay, my friend. You must be in pain with all this moving around," Sam responded, but Khalil moaned again.

Alex walked over and sat next to him where he was now lying on the bed.

"You're trying to tell us something, aren't you, Khalil?"

Khalil's eyes declared relief as he nodded.

Sam rummaged through the countless books and papers that lay scattered on the floor and eventually found a pen and a newspaper.

Since his writing hand's arm was in a cast they watched as Khalil took great effort to write a note with his other hand—of which two fingers were in a splint. The note simply said *clothes.* Sam leaped across to where he had dropped the hospital bag, that carried Khalil's clothes, on the floor by the front door. He emptied the bag onto the bed next to Khalil whose hand immediately searched for and pulled his pants from the pile. With his two broken digits, he clumsily wriggled his hand inside the pockets—first one and then the other. When his hand came out empty from both pockets, he frantically went back to the first pocket.

"What is it, Khalil? What are you looking for?" Alex asked, taking the pants from him. She stuck her hand into the pocket and pulled out a small scrunched up patch of navy-blue cloth. Khalil groaned with exhaustion and dropped his head back onto the pillow, closing his eyes as he did so.

Alex inspected the piece of crumpled fabric which was glued together by dried blood. As her fingers pulled the fabric fibers apart she flipped it over.

"What is it?" Sam asked as his head turned sideways to make sense of the image.

CHAPTER TWELVE

"I'm not entirely sure yet. There's too much blood."

Fabric in hand she dashed into the small kitchenette and wet the piece of cloth under the tap. The blood dissolved and revealed a partial image that might have once been a white square or a rectangle. Inside the space was one half of a bright red, circle shape with two smaller ones floating on either side of it and below it a word—or what was left of one after it had been torn away from the rest of the image.

"It's a logo! Khalil, you're a genius!" she yelled when she placed it flat on the table in front of Sam and Father Rob, smoothing it out with her hand.

"Something tells me that's exactly how you broke those two fingers of yours, mate," Sam joked. "Our brave friend had the presence of mind to rip it off one of his attackers' clothing," he added.

"It appears to be a company logo but it's only part of it. It looks like it's something *tech*," Alex said.

From where Father Rob stared at it upside down, he pointed to the barely noticeable image in one of the corners. "That looks like a Chinese letter."

Alex flipped the patch upside down. "Why am I not surprised?"

"Does it mean something to you?" Father Rob frowned at Alex's blasé response.

"I guess you can say that. We had an encounter with a few Chinese men ourselves and they seemed to have had access to enough technology to track us down in the middle of the Adriatic Sea.

"That and the fact that they had Chinese military issue weapons," Sam added, taking a seat opposite her at the table.

"I'm confused," Father Rob said as he also took a seat at the table. "Are you saying the Turkish government is conspiring with the Chinese government? Against us?"

Alex rubbed the piece of fabric between her fingers.

"We're not saying anything, Father. We don't have any proof that the Turks are behind this. What we do know, however, is that the Chinese are somehow involved," Sam answered.

"More importantly, it begs the question as to why a tech company would be after the manna," Alex said while still trying to make sense of the fabric between her fingers.

"They had sophisticated military guns, drones, and the ability to track us. Perhaps weapons?"

"Then why are they after the manna? That makes no sense," Father Rob said.

Alex didn't answer. Instead she continued rubbing her fingers over the patch of fabric, feeling and sensing her way through a maze of questions that searched her mind for answers. Sam took his turn inspecting the fabric, running his fingers, in much the same way as his wife had, over the logo.

"I'm no fashionista but I don't think I'm far off thinking this cloth isn't just any ordinary piece of clothing fabric. It's almost as if it's a piece of strong tissue paper yet it's nothing like tissue paper at all," Sam commented when he scrunched up the ripped patch between his fingers and watched it bounce back uncreased. "And it's really thick and strong," he added.

"I think I know of someone who might be able to tell us about this piece of fabric," Alex announced, "and I think we ought to take Khalil with us."

Forty minutes later Father Rob dropped them off behind the church and made his way back to the front of the basilica in time to prepare for evening mass. Alex and Sam carried Khalil into his cousin's tailor shop and like before, Yusuf sat in front of his sewing machine in the corner. As was to be expected, Yusuf wasn't at all pleased with their visit when he saw his cousin's battered and bruised body enter his shop.

"I knew getting involved with you was going to get him killed!

What have you done?" he yelled at them, taking Alex's place under Khalil's broken arm.

"He's not dead, Yusuf. In fact, your cousin saved a boy's life. He's a brave man," Alex retorted.

"He should've never helped you out in the first place. He has a family, you know."

"We're aware," was all Alex decided to say so as to not antagonize Yusuf any further.

Yusuf beckoned for Alex to open a door that led into the back of the shop before a small set of stairs deposited them inside an even darker room in the attic. Alex allowed her eyes to take in the tiny space. A single mattress lay on top of two wooden pallets on the floor in one corner. Next to it an upside-down vegetable crate acted as his nightstand, displaying a Bible and a small lamp. Barely five feet away a single wooden chair served as a table upon which a few mismatched dirty dishes were stacked. Next to it, two more crates along the wall served as a kitchen counter holding a single burner stove and an old kettle. In the opposite corner a low three-drawer dresser separated a humble restroom from the living area and next to it stood a bucket with a towel draped over it.

Yusuf was still mumbling words in his native tongue that were no doubt unsavory, as he and Sam gently lay Khalil down onto his bed.

"It's important that you keep him hidden, Yusuf," Sam ventured with caution.

"Hidden from who? He needs a doctor," Yusuf argued.

"No, he doesn't. I am a doctor and I've done what was necessary. They won't be able to keep him safe. Your cousin's life depends on it, Yusuf. When the IV runs out you can remove the needle and feed him broth and water. Keep him hydrated and lying still and he'll be fine. You can give him liquid painkillers if he needs it," Sam instructed.

"You need to leave," Yusuf said sternly, pushing both Alex and Sam towards the stairs.

"Actually, we need your help," Alex dared to ask.

"Help? You're crazy if you think I'm going to help you. Don't you think you've done enough? You need to stay away from us." Yusuf flicked his hands in the way you might chase a stray dog off your lawn.

"It's important. It might help us find the men who did this to Khalil," Alex said again, holding out the piece of torn off fabric.

"What can you tell us about this?"

"Nothing, now go away," Yusuf said abruptly.

"Look carefully, Yusuf, please? It's important," Alex urged.

Yusuf looked back at his cousin whose eyes urged him to help. He reluctantly snatched the piece of fabric from her hand and walked over to his nightstand. He took his time inspecting the fabric under the small yellow light before he shoved it back in her hand.

"It's a fire-retardant fabric you'd usually find in a laboratory or chemical factory. That's all I know. I've never seen the logo, or what's left of it, but I can tell you that it was embroidered by an industrial machine and that the red cotton is custom-made."

"So a uniform?" Sam checked.

"Probably, yes."

"Thank you, Yusuf. That helps us a great deal. Look after our friend." Sam shook his hand before he and Alex left.

B ack at their yacht Alex flipped open her laptop and searched the internet for Chinese tech companies with a logo that looked remotely like the partial imprint on the fabric patch. Sam had motored the yacht a fair way from the small marina as they usually did when they settled in for the night. He slid into the kitchen next to Alex and ran his eyes over the laptop's screen.

"Anything?"

"Nothing. Most of the tech companies with red logos are all IT based or vehicle manufacturing plants. And none have these odd-looking balls in the logo either."

"You're assuming it came from an overall. It could just as well have come from a collared shirt's pocket." It dawned on them that they'd never bothered to ask Yusuf. Not that he would've been able to communicate it properly anyway.

"Well," Alex said, "the Internet only gives us so much to work with. Perhaps it's something we need to do in person."

"You mean fly to China."

Alex didn't answer. Her eyes confirmed Sam's supposition.

"And this is why I love you so much. Never scared to take the bull by its horns," Sam said with pride, and got up to pour them each a cup of coffee before he spoke again. "There are one and a half billion people in China though and who knows how many tech companies? Where would we even start? Beijing?"

"I have no idea, Sam. It could be anywhere, but we have to start somewhere, and right now, this is the only lead we have. They said they'd contact us with further instructions, but they haven't. Perhaps they've found us useless, I don't know. But what I do know is that we can't just sit here and wait for better days."

"Let's hope you're right. Question is, what are we going to do once we find the company? Have you thought of that yet?"

She hadn't. "We'll figure it out. We always do."

Sam walked over and lifted away the grid in front of one of the ventilation ducts in the wall to retrieve a small black bag. He plonked the compact backpack onto the table and scanned through the contents of passports, cash and a few burner phones before placing it back into the zip pouch inside the bag. They unclipped the magazines from their guns and locked them away inside the concealed safe in the kitchen, aware of the fact that China had some of the strictest gun regulations in the world.

"Hopefully we won't need them anyway," Alex remarked when Sam took a deep breath as he locked the safe.

"Well, as they say, no time like the present," he said, masking his inner anxiety in his usual flippant tone before heading toward the flybridge. Whilst he was not ignorant to the fact that men didn't possess the proverbial female sixth sense, he certainly couldn't shake the alarm bells that had gone off in the pit of his stomach. Every cell in his body wanted to turn away rather than go ahead, but they had silently agreed to avenge the priest's murder and complete Stavros' mission to find the manna. Quitting wasn't an option.

Still deep in thought, Sam was climbing the steel ladder onto the flybridge when he felt the hard blow to his back, fell from the ladder and landed heavily on the main deck., Alex, packing a few items of clothing in their carry-on bags in their berth, stopped as she heard the thud overhead. With her senses heightened she leaped across the small cabin to the porthole but saw nothing. Instinctively she reached for the gun at her waist, only to recall they had just locked it away. Her eyes searched both nightstands for a fallback weapon and settled on the bug spray. It would do. Armed only with the aerosol tin she fell back against the inside wall by the doorway and popped her head out for a quick view into the hull. It was clear. She proceeded cautiously through the sitting area and kitchen, picking up a knife in passing. Sounds of something being dragged across the deck above her followed by several footsteps sent her senses into high alert.

With her eyes on the doorway she allowed her free hand to find the safe and only looked away briefly to enter the digital combination. She ran her fingers nervously over the first four numbers of the code before everything went black around her.

CHAPTER THIRTEEN

The noxious sweet smell of benzene splashing in his face woke Sam up. A reflex had him open his eyes but he instantly forced them shut as the liquid burned his eyes. He fought for fresh air in his lungs and turned his head away as another splash of fluid hit his chest. Attempting to wipe his face he realized his hands were tied behind his back. He spat out some of the gasoline that had managed to find its way into his mouth and tried to wipe his eyes on his shoulder, only to realize his shirt was also soaked in the petrol. Unable to see, he homed his hearing in on the snickering male voices somewhere in front of him. There were at least two, he deduced, as he expelled another ball of petrol-tinged saliva in their direction. He recognized the sound of liquid hitting the insides of an almost empty metal container followed by the liquid splashing out onto the floor. He took note of the fact that the sound grew more distant with each splash, signifying that it was being moved away from him. He turned his head and heightened his senses in search of Alex but heard nothing. Behind him his bound hands felt the hardness of a steel pole against his back. His wedding ring chimed against the pole as he felt his way around it until his fingers settled on the familiar soft cotton ropes from their yacht. He must still be on the yacht, he concluded with relief while his insides remained tense over Alex's safety. Still unable to see he slowly turned his head, allowing his ears to determine his exact position on the yacht. Behind him the hollow noise of an empty metal container hitting the floor startled him. Moments later he heard a metal lid pop off a new canister before the petrol splashed against something. Alex coughed and gasped behind Sam, bringing him a strange twisted sense of relief. She was still alive, albeit in the same unfortunate situation he found himself in.

"Alex! I'm over here!" he yelled to put her at ease.

Still recovering from the gasoline dousing, Alex didn't answer. But as long as Sam heard her cough and draw oxygen into her lungs he was satisfied.

Sam's bold disruption to communicate with her must have angered their captors as his face was struck by the sole of someone's boot. The metallic taste of blood flooded his mouth. He tried to open his eyes again. The blurry outlines of the stern of the yacht slowly came into vision in front of him. Again his fingers wrapped around the steel pole behind him for confirmation. He had been tied to the ladder beneath the flybridge. That meant they were both on the main deck and Alex would be in the seating area. He turned his head to the right over his shoulder and as far back as his body would allow in an attempt to see her. His eyes still stung from the petrol, causing him to blink several times before her faint silhouette came into sight where she was lying on the main deck. Desperate to cry out to her he refrained; for fear of arousing further hostility from their captors who had just thrown the second empty jerry can aside. Instead he coughed; so she'd know he was okay. After a slight pause he heard her cough in reply. She was okay too, for now.

With his vision not yet fully restored, it was too hard to see properly, even with the light from the flybridge above him, but it afforded just enough illumination across the main deck for him to see three men—two on board the yacht, and one more seated next to the engine in a small fishing dinghy floating next to the aft side. The oars dangling from the sides of the boat indicated how they had managed to sneak up on them. Sam twisted his hands in an effort to loosen the ropes around his wrists as he waited for their next move.

The deck seating afforded Alex much needed protection from the attackers' field of vision where they stood at the stern. Using it to her full advantage, Alex wriggled her body across the deck and in doing so, drenched her clothes further with gasoline. Aside from her lungs burning as she inhaled the strong fumes her eyesight was clear. Her hands were bound, so were her feet. When she reached the inward curve of the built-in seating behind her, she used her elbows and pushed herself up onto the white cushions. It was quite evident that the attackers were not experienced at all, not having tied her hands behind her back. Perhaps they assumed her being a woman posed no threat. They underestimated her, she thought. From behind the backrest she peered over the cushions and saw Sam propped up against the ladder. Two of the men were already inside the small boat preparing to leave while the third appeared to be sending a text from his phone. She ducked down into the seating and moved her fingers nimbly over the knots around her ankles. The rope sprang free with very little effort. Using her teeth she set about the knots around her wrists having to pause a few times to rid her mouth of the bitter chemical taste that seeped into her mouth. The ropes around her wrists were harder to untie and clung together under the moisture of the flammable liquid she had been soaked with. She heard one of the men talking and carefully popped her head back over the cushion to see him speaking on his cellphone. He was speaking Chinese. Her eyes trailed to one of the men in the boat who promptly passed a cigarette lighter, along with a small, rounded white object, to his associate with the phone who had remained on the yacht. Alex dropped back behind the backrest and bit down harder onto the rope between her hands; realizing the object was a candle. Ignoring the bitter taste in her mouth her teeth worked relentlessly through the tight bindings until a final tug released the last knot. With the men now preoccupied with completing their mission, Alex took the opportunity to descend below deck. Again a mistake on their part to have left her so close to the doorway. Her heart beat fiercely against her chest when her fingers punched the digital sequence into the safe. She'd have to be careful, she thought. A bullet into the fuel on deck would set the entire boat ablaze, along with her and Sam. The door popped open and she worked quickly, reloading her Glock before putting it in its usual place under her shirt in the small of her back.

Suddenly aware that she could no longer hear the man's voice on the phone, she assumed he had set the boat on fire and left, but then decided she would've smelled the smoke. She didn't. Her mind went to their getaway bag which she quickly snatched from its hiding place and slipped it into her waistband underneath her shirt. Adrenaline pumped through her veins as she suddenly thought to cut Sam's ropes instead of wasting time fumbling with the knots. In a last effort of planning she spun around to reach for the knife that lay on the kitchen counter behind her but instead, found herself staring down the barrel of the man on the phone's gun.

There was no mistaking the short syllables that issued from his mouth as being a warning. It sounds the same regardless of the language it's said in. Alex held her hands up in surrender. They had mistaken her for a timid woman before and it had served her well, at least until now. She whimpered the way B-list actresses do in the low-grade movies and begged for her life. His eyes fell on the knife that lay on the counter behind her, setting off a new sequence of short, abrupt words while his gun motioned for her to move away from the counter. She complied. She still had her gun and so far he was none the wiser. He pushed the gun into her back between her shoulder blades, shoving her towards the stairs to go up onto the deck, and she again let out a fake whimper, then coughed. She knew Sam would be within earshot and translate it that she was still in control. The Chinese man trailed behind her, shouting for her to move, so she did. When her feet hit the last of the four steps before she reached the main deck, using her elevated position over him, she kicked backward and disarmed her assailant. As she spun around she kicked him across the face, affording her enough time to pull her gun out and pin it against his forehead.

"Move!" she instructed in a low stern voice as she swung him around. These men were inexperienced, yes, but she wasn't about to take any chances. With her Glock pinned firmly against the base of his skull, she wrapped her arm around his neck in a headlock and climbed the stairs with him. When they reached the top she tightened her elbow onto his wind-pipe and moved her gun's barrel to his temple. Using his body as a shield she moved along the deck towards where Sam was still sitting against the ladder.

"That didn't take you long," Sam said with glee, humored by the shocked expressions of the two Chinese associates on the boat. Quite unexpectedly the tables had turned for them as they now watched their ringleader under threat of being killed. Alex moved in front of Sam, setting up a barrier of protection between their guns and Sam. She pushed her gun deeper into her hostage's temple and told him to instruct his associates to put their guns down. She knew he understood English, all Chinese did. He ignored her. Alex tightened her grip around his neck and moved her gun down to his thigh.

"I don't have to kill you to make you talk, you know," she warned him, pushing the barrel firmly into his hamstring.

It did the trick and a few short commands left his mouth, after which his men dropped their guns at their feet.

"I hate to be a party-pooper but I think it's time to blow out the birthday candle," Sam announced as he pushed his chin toward the flickering light in the middle of the deck ahead of them.

It wasn't only her eyes on the candle. The two men in the boat had their eyes pinned on it too, and with good reason, since the wax was burning away faster than any of them would've liked at that point.

"Tell them to extinguish the candle," Alex commanded her hostage, this time forcing the gun into the soft spot above his ear. He complied immediately with no additional effort required. His men, on the other hand, did not and he barked his staccato words once more. Again they ignored him. Alex turned her gun onto his men.

"Do as he says or I'll kill you both!" she yelled.

The two men exchanged glances and, as if their ringleader sensed their next move, he barked another command at his men. Under her grasp, Alex sensed he was angry at his men's blatant insubordination. The words had barely left his mouth when his suspicions came to pass and he stood stunned as he watched his men speed off in the boat, leaving their ringleader captive in the hands of the enemy.

CHAPTER FOURTEEN

S am hissed one long whistle between his teeth. "Now that's a stab in the back if ever I've seen one."

The stupefied look on their prisoner's face declared that he too hadn't seen it coming. Alex felt the man's shoulders droop beneath her grip as his body reacted to the shame and calamity his men had brought upon him. In the midst of the new situation they now faced, the candle flickered back and forth in the gentle late evening breeze, its flame coming dangerously close to the deck on far too many occasions. Out of time and not willing to tempt fate any further, Alex executed the strangling technique she had acquired through her special forces training on their now prisoner. Ten seconds later she let the man fall unconscious to the floor at her feet. With their immediate threat now deactivated she leaped across the deck and extinguished the burning candle before turning back to free Sam.

"I wonder how many times you still have to save my life," he said as she worked her way through the knots.

"Probably as many times as you have to save mine," Alex replied when her fingers slipped through the last knot around Sam's wrists.

"What cowards would leave their leader for dead like this?" Sam asked as he started peeling his petrol-soaked clothing from his body.

"The inexperienced kind," Alex answered as she dropped her clothing on the floor too. "These guys were either complete imbeciles or total novices, not to mention the fact that they think women don't possess a brain," she added.

"I'm inclined to think they're equally idiotic and inexperienced. But the real question is, who are they working for?"

"Well, this time we have leverage and a source. Unlike our previous attackers, this guy is very much alive, and if I have my way with him, he'll rat them out in no time. Besides, once he wakes up and recalls what happened, he'll want revenge," Alex said as she disappeared below to take a shower and put on fresh clothes.

"Okay, don't worry about the half dead guy on our deck. You just keep knocking them over and I'll keep cleaning up the mess," Sam said with playful sarcasm as he looked down at the unconscious man lying at his feet.

After they'd washed the flammable liquid from the deck, Alex and Sam had both dozed off where they were keeping guard next to their prisoner. They had tied him up to the very ladder Sam had been secured to, taking extra precautions with a set of handcuffs. It was in the early hours of the morning when the metal against metal sound of his handcuffs woke Alex. She watched silently as he wrestled in a futile attempt to free himself, wondering if he thought he could swim the three miles back to shore if he was successful in his escape. With the next loud clanging sound, Sam woke and spotted the amused expression on Alex's face. Letting it play out he eventually cleared his throat, startling their prisoner who didn't find humor in the situation when he soon realized they'd been watching him squirm for some time already.

"No, please don't let us stop you," Sam said sarcastically and sat back as if he was readying himself for the start of a film.

The man mumbled something in his native tongue under his breath.

"Yes, yes, we get it. You're a little upset that your friends could just leave you behind like that. Spare us the pity party and tell us who hired you," Alex jumped straight in.

"What, no coffee first?" Sam mocked, further annoying their Chinese prisoner.

Even though the man's lips were pursed with anger, two tight white lines that were clearly visible in even the faintest of dawn light, he wasn't about to talk. Yes, he'd been festering about the very betrayal since he woke, but he was no rat.

Alex stretched, disappeared downstairs and soon reappeared with two coffees, adding to the man's torture.

"Right, shall we start again?" she asked as she took a sip of coffee.

"Tell you what, since I consider myself fair and all, I'll start with an easy question. How about you tell us your name?" She placed her cup down on the table and stared directly into his face where he sat cuffed to the ladder on the floor. The man didn't answer.

"When were you last around a woman when she wakes up before sunrise, mate? I wouldn't mess this one around if I were you. She's not what I'd call a morning person, if you know what I mean," Sam cautioned him over the brim of his cup.

Alex stared the man down and between her forceful gaze and Sam's casual warning, the man finally succumbed.

"Chen Zhao," he mumbled.

"Now that wasn't so hard was it?" Alex mocked taking another sip of coffee before commencing a sequence of questions. "And where might you be from, Chen Zhao?"

Again he contemplated not answering before replying.

"Dongguan."

"And where exactly is Dongguan?"

"South China, near Hong Kong." Chen had no trouble answering now.

"Who do you work for, Chen?"

"I don't work for anyone," he said.

"What about your friends? If you can even call them friends. I'd call them cowards," Sam interjected.

Chen spat out into the air and mumbled something in Chinese.

"English, mate, we don't understand a word you're saying," Sam spoke again.

"Why were you trying to kill us? Who gave you the orders?" Alex continued the questioning.

Chen squeezed his lips together and turned his face away from them. Alex didn't say a word in response. Instead she disappeared below deck again and came back with a freshly boiled kettle which she plonked on the table in front of them. Just to be certain he knew what could happen, she slowly added the hot water to her cup, allowing the steam to wisp into the air. Sam cleared his throat, drawing Chen's attention to the steaming hot water display.

"Let's try this again, shall we? Why were you trying to kill us and who gave you the orders?"

Chen's eyes were pinned to the kettle of steaming water on the table, but as if to call her bluff, he still didn't answer. Alex rose, lifted the kettle from the table and moved closer to where Chen had already curled his body into a ball. Alex didn't budge. She tipped the kettle over and allowed a thin steady flow of boiling water to run onto the deck close to his bare feet—they had removed his shoes while he was sleeping. A tiny splatter of hot water splashed onto his ankle causing him to instantly pull away. Alex stopped. It was a taster. She stared him down, yet he kept quiet. He was an imbecile, she thought as she went down on her haunches and tipped the kettle over once more, this time directly above his head. Intentionally missing his head, she allowed the small stream of water to trickle down past his ear and onto his shoulder. Tricking him into thinking that it was a simple misjudgment on her part and that he wouldn't be as lucky when she corrected her mistake, should be enough to frighten him into talking. Her tactical theatrics paid off when the burning sting soaked through Chen's shirt onto his skin.

"Okay, okay!" he screamed.

Alex paused.

"I don't know who he is. He only spoke to me via phone," Chen divulged.

Alex got up and stared out to where the sun cast its bright orange blanket over the horizon. He hadn't had the phone on him when they'd searched his pockets. The cowards must have taken it with them. She turned back to face him again.

"What exactly were your orders?"

"He wants the liquid. That's all I know, I swear!"

"The liquid from the bones," Alex clarified.

Chen nodded.

"Did he say why?"

Chen shook his head.

"How much was he willing to pay for it?"

"One hundred thousand American dollars."

"And, as it stands, you don't have the manna nor know who does," she continued.

"We have no idea where it is. He was convinced you had it, because you were with the boy. Now, no one knows where it is."

"And the priest? Did you murder the priest?" Sam questioned.

"No. That wasn't us."

Alex stared out across the ocean again.

"Does the number forty-nine mean anything to you?"

Chen suddenly looked up. His eyes moved between the kettle and Alex's gaze.

"So you do know what it means," she confirmed.

"I think it's still hot, mate," Sam nudged, referring to the kettle Chen's eyes now fixed on. He sighed but changed from his curled-up position and stretched his legs out before he answered.

"The Fangs," Chen reluctantly declared.

"What's that?" Sam asked.

"You have the same burn mark on your right wrist as the dead guy who came before you." Alex spoke, her words having the exact effect she had hoped for.

Chen shuffled restlessly as his mind digested the death threat.

"The Hong Kong Fangs."

"So it's a gang?" Sam clarified.

Chen nodded, visibly annoyed with himself for giving up the information without much of a fight.

"So the numbers are identifiers?" Alex reasoned out loud.

Chen nodded again.

"Excellent. You did great, Chen," she mocked. "So here's how it's going to go. You're going to tell us everything we need to know about the Hong Kong Fangs. Where they operate from, what they do, everything. Got it?"

"I'm as good as dead if I tell you," Chen argued.

"Well, I might be wrong, my friend, but your gangster friends left you to die, so I'm guessing they think you're probably dead already."

Chen didn't look pleased.

"Why the long face, mate? That's great news for you... and us, if you think about it. If you're already dead, they won't come for you. It's a win-win!" Sam exclaimed.

"They know everything and their eyes are everywhere. There's no escaping them, believe me," Chen scoffed. "You have no idea who you're dealing with, trust me. All three of us are as good as dead."

"You're assuming they're after us," said Alex.

Chen broke into a nervous laughter, declaring just how deep his fear for the Fangs ran.

"They are! There's a bounty on your heads and they won't stop until they see your corpses and, thanks to you, mine too. They're like a Mexican cartel and Italian mafia all rolled into one. They're everywhere from the east to the west and everywhere in between, operating in cells while receiving full police protection."

"So that explains your military issue QBZs and the drone," Sam inferred.

"And why they're able to track our every move," Alex added.

"You'll never make it out of here alive, fancy yacht or not," Chen declared.

From where Alex had been standing watching the sunrise, she paced across the deck and looked Chen squarely in the eyes.

"And that, my friend, is exactly where you come in. You are going to make contact with your connections and find a way of getting us into China safely."

CHAPTER FIFTEEN

C hen vehemently opposed going along with Alex and Sam's plan for him to conspire against the Fangs. In his mind it wasn't even a case of principles over ratting his clan members out, it was fear for his life and what they'd do to him long before they eventually killed him. But Alex and Sam were relentless and Chen soon realized they'd probably kill him otherwise—albeit a far more merciful death. So when he finally gave up the fight he took the burner phone Sam handed him. As if he needed any further persuasion from them, Sam looked him squarely in the eyes.

"Let's get one thing straight, Chen. If you as much as breathe the wrong way or pull any sneaky moves, I'll do more than pour a kettle of hot water over your head. Got it?"

Sam's warning was nothing more than a bluff, of course, but Chen didn't need to know that. If they were going to trust this man to get them into China, they'd have to make certain he feared them.

Chen nodded while his shaky fingers moved through the buttons on the phone. A brief but serious conversation, under Sam's penetrating stare, followed before he delivered the phone back into Sam's hands.

"All set?" Sam asked Chen.

"Yes. My man will meet us in Split."

"When?" Alex asked.

"Midnight tonight."

Alex glanced at her watch and then, with slight trepidation, at Sam.

"Don't worry, we'll be there. By my reckoning it's about nine hours by boat from here. If we don't run into any more surprises, we'll have plenty of time to get there before midnight. I just hope for your sake your 'man' can be trusted, Chen," Sam added.

"I trust him with my life. He's high-ranked and has many influential connections in the group and besides, he owes me a favor for saving his sister's life some time back. He'll come through for me." Chen raised his chin as he spoke the last sentence, but not just for his captors' benefit. After the last betrayal he was desperate to believe that he still had at least one person he could trust.

. . .

The trip northbound across the Adriatic towards Croatia went smoothly, at least for the most part. The underwater riptides along the coastline proved much stronger than Sam had anticipated. As a result, to avoid capsizing where the gusts pushed the yacht sideways, he was forced to zig-zag the yacht across, which unfortunately added a substantial amount of hours to their traveling time. Deciding that Chen's dark gray military outfit would certainly give away the situation, Alex had him change into some of Sam's clothes. Almost half Sam's size, the clothes hung loosely on his body but, cleaned up and dressed in civilian clothes, it erased all evidence that he had set up their meeting under duress and was about to smuggle two Brits into China.

It took a little more than twelve hours for them to eventually reach the small port of Divulje in Split. "You ready?" Sam asked Alex in the kitchen below deck.

"As ready as I'll ever be. At least we're in a position to retain our weapons since it's fair to say we're gaining illegal passage into China. That's if Chen's contact knows what he's doing and doesn't also pull a fast one on him. Once we're in, we don't need Chen anymore."

She loaded both Glocks and passed one to Sam before hiding her Beretta in its usual place inside her ankle boot. She always made certain she carried an auxiliary weapon.

"Where are we meeting the guy?"

"Behind some restaurant or bar at the end of the jetty. Come on, Alex, we need to go." It was close to midnight by the time they stepped off the yacht.

S ince it wasn't quite the summer season yet, the midnight air was crisp against their faces as Alex and Sam walked alongside Chen toward their meeting point. Apart from the four moored sailing yachts and one empty ferry, the port was completely deserted. Not trusting the desolate location, Sam had cuffed Chen's wrist to his, as insurance. The tide pushed the humble jetty across the water, making it slightly more challenging to walk along, but they soon stepped off onto dry land in Croatia. Chen paused and trailed his eyes along the shore.

"There," Chen pointed towards the small restaurant that sat a bit further along the road next to the harbor wall.

With only a few soft red lights that illuminated the large name sign on the pitched roof and one small yellow lamp that hung at the front door, it looked nothing more than a derelict timber shack. It was already closed for the night and there wasn't a person in sight. Further away the only three street-lights cast long shadows across the empty parking area that was flanked by open lots on both sides. Their feet crunched noisily on the small brown pebbles that lay scattered across the surface of the dirt road leading up to the distressed timber building. In the distance behind them the rigging of the moored yachts chimed against their masts, amplified by the offshore wind that pushed into them from behind. As they approached the dark shadows behind the restaurant, Alex rested her hand on her gun in the small of her back. Chen whistled a quick multi-tone tune to announce their arrival and moments later a similar whistle answered back. With her hand still on her gun, Alex tightened her grip on the handle, feeling the hard steel etch into her palm.

"We're good. He's here," Chen announced as he came to a halt.

From the shadows behind the building, the petite figure of a bald Chinese man emerged, his appearance in total contrast to what they had expected. With a broad smile and overly dramatic embrace he greeted Chen, kissing him on each cheek. It was as if they had just been welcomed into his home for a party and were about to be offered welcome drinks. His exuberant, cheerful personality was not at all what Alex and Sam had expected a member of a dangerous Chinese criminal organization would be like. Adorned with chunky gold chains around his neck and colorful gemstone rings on all ten of his fingers, he resembled a petite Chinese version of Liberace. He wore a red satin work shirt—unbuttoned down to his navel, to show off his jewelry no doubt, since he didn't have much of a physique—and mustard yellow pants with white snakeskin loafers. Making no attempt at all to hide the fact that he was armed, a shiny gold semi-automatic pistol was on full display, tucked into the front of his waistband. He noticed the shared handcuffs and immediately stuck his hands between Sam and Chen's shoulders, parting the men like he was preparing to dive into a pool between them. Without a moment's notice he rapidly drew his gun as if he was John Wayne himself and fired a shot through the chain before Alex or Sam even knew what was coming.

"There, now we can trust each other," he announced, before putting his arm around Chen's shoulders to turn and walk him toward a black limousine that was parked around the other side of the restaurant.

Still stunned by how quickly this unlikely-looking gangster had drawn his gun, Alex and Sam followed them and settled into the vehicle's luxury white leather seats. Sam noted the gold initials printed on each of the headrests and the floor mats. It simply read *JM*. It shouted luxury and money until the moment the doors closed and the entire limousine's interior transformed into bright fluorescent pink and blue lights. It was as if they were inside a seedy nightclub. Chen and his contact, who still hadn't introduced himself, entered into jubilant conversation in Chinese, laughing as if they were sharing bad jokes.

As the limousine pulled away, Alex and Sam sat watching the two men who were seated opposite them in stunned surprise. Entirely ignored by both men they were grateful that it was just a short drive to the Split airport. They'd expected to be dropped off at the main entrance, but instead, the chauffeur drove in by way of a separate gate and onto the tarmac before the limo stopped and let them out next to a private long-range jet. Still Chen and his friend continued their private party as, arms around shoulders, they ascended into the private plane. Feeling like they were the miserable wallflowers at a boisterous college party, Alex and Sam followed the duo inside without saying a word.

But, as if they had all just entered through a secret portal into the deep underworld of Satan, the petite Chinese man's entire personality suddenly changed. In one fell swoop, his laughter and cheery demeanor transformed into a steely expressionless being whose black eyes conveyed dominance and intimidation. The light and cheerful nightclub atmosphere from the limousine was instantly replaced by a cold and rigid space that had Alex and Sam stiffen with vigilance. His cold eyes locked onto his guests as they sat in the tan-colored luxury leather seats opposite him, speaking without as much as blinking.

"Did they hurt you, Chen?"

Instantly reminded of his colleague's prominence and now finding himself plunged into an awkward position, Chen replied with a faint denial. It would have been so easy for him to say the contrary and have Alex and Sam killed on the spot. Yet he knew, in a roundabout unofficial way, that Alex and Sam would be his only protection from being hunted down and killed by the Fangs. He had seen it firsthand; treason did not sit well with them, and if he was to have any chance of making it back into China alive, he'd have to stick with the lesser enemy of the two.

Even now, pinned under the man's steely black eyes, Alex and Sam didn't allow his evil stares to intimidate them, regardless of the sudden fear that gripped their insides. They were instantly aware just how much authority this man had, but they also knew it wouldn't be the last time they faced evil.

"Great! Then let's get the party started! I'm Jin Mu, by the way, but everyone calls me Moo-Moo," he smiled with pride, and, now visible in the bright lights above his head, a gold canine tooth glistened.

And just like that, as if his party personality pushed his evil one aside, the effervescent Chinese Liberace was back.

A lex and Sam remained vigilant throughout the entire flight. They took turns sleeping and politely declined any food and drinks on offer, just in case it was laced. Now, more convinced than ever, they couldn't allow themselves to drop their guard, not even for one second. They had experienced the instantaneous schizophrenic episodes of their host personally and it was very evident Jin Mu wouldn't hesitate to kill them in an instant for whatever reasons he might deem fit. Chen eventually fell asleep until the jet's wheels touched down onto the small private airfield just outside Hong Kong.

CHAPTER SIXTEEN

"You're on your own now," Chen announced to Alex and Sam as they stepped out onto the tarmac at Shek Kong Airfield; Chen a few feet in front of Alex and Sam while Jin Mu was on the phone in the plane.

A quick glance at the hangars across the landing strip revealed several military soldiers moving around. Alex stiffened and drew Sam's attention to the estimated dozen men at work all across the small airport. Sam quickened his pace and gripped Chen's arm just above his elbow, bringing him to a halt.

"Not so fast Chen. What's all this?" Sam spoke sternly but in a subdued voice.

"It's our airfield."

"It's a bloody military base and you know it," Sam said angrily.

"I got you to China safely. That was our deal. You're on your own," Chen repeated with sudden boldness, breaking his arm free from Sam's grip.

"Do we have a problem?" Jin Mu suddenly asked from where he stood in the door of the small plane behind them.

"Well, do we?" Chen said with a cocky tone as he looked up into Sam's eyes. He was using Jin Mu and the military base's protection to his full advantage.

"Let's go, Sam," Alex intervened before adding, "you better hope our paths don't cross again, Chen. Tell your boss to call off the dogs."

Chen scoffed in reply as Alex and Sam turned and walked away. The landing strip was flanked by two grassed areas on either side, and in turn, each one was lined with a row of large trees before it bordered onto a small industrial neighborhood. On the other side of the trees in front of them was a narrow road that led away from the airfield. To their right were three hangars and a small fleet of army vehicles, a helicopter and two small four-seater planes.

"That way," Alex pointed, choosing the shortest route across the grass and between the trees to, what they hoped would be, their exit.

They ignored the suspicious stares from a few army men as they passed them, keeping their heads down. But it wasn't enough when two armed men suddenly pulled up in an army Jeep and stopped them. Incapable of understanding them and acting purely on the assumption that they obviously queried their presence, Sam turned and pointed to where Chen and Jin Mu were in conversation behind them.

"We're with them," Sam tried.

Without warning, as Sam, Alex and the two soldiers watched, Jin Mu's quick-draw of his golden gun impressed them once more when he fired a single gunshot into Chen's chest. As Chen dropped to his knees, and the two soldiers watched unconcerned, Jin Mu finished him off with a final bullet to his head. Sudden fear ripped through Alex and Sam when Jin Mu nodded at the two soldiers. His silent orders had both soldiers instantly move forward to seize Alex and Sam. Quick to react and avoid being captured, Sam swung the first punch, hitting one of the soldiers across the jaw before he even had time to raise his weapon. He quickly followed through with a second fisted blow which rendered the slight-framed soldier unconscious on the ground. Alex had done the same with the second soldier whose movements were almost swift enough for him to fully draw his gun. She thrust her fist into his throat and finished him off with an uppercut before he could even blink.

Jin Mu's voice echoed across the airfield followed by a quick succession of bullets from his gun. Unlike his John Wayne draw, his aim left much to be desired, sending a number of bullets several feet away from them into the grass and trees. He barked across the runway, sending more soldiers storming towards Alex and Sam.

"Get in!" Alex yelled for Sam as she slipped behind the wheel of the army Jeep. Heading directly for the trees and the exit road, the Jeep bounced its way over the grassed area. More shots flew by their heads, loudly ricocheting off the Jeep's steel frame. She swerved as two more military vehicles tried to cut them off. Forced to change direction as the soldiers moved in on them, she pushed the Jeep through a nearby empty hangar, sending a mechanic's tool trolley flying through the air. Out the other side the tires screeched around the bend as she navigated the vehicle back towards the exit but was forced to rapidly adjust direction when a small fleet of vehicles blocked off their path. Their eyes frantically searched for another way out as more bullets hit the sides of the Jeep. In the rear mirror Alex watched a fleet of vehicles chase after them. In front of them, the small military base narrowed to a close about a hundred yards further on. They were running out of options. To their right the runway lay bare, except for Jin Mu's jet that hadn't moved from its landing place. A sudden quick-witted notion had Alex slam on the brakes while she turned in between two hangars before her foot flattened the accelerator and she gunned the Jeep in the direction of Jin Mu's plane. With him directly in the line of fire, the soldiers ceased their gunfire, affording Alex and Sam the perfect opportunity to speed across the runway past the plane. With Jin Mu's plane now behind them she gained speed as she pushed the Jeep across to the other side of the runway before disappearing between the lush trees. Still in pursuit, the army vehicles followed a fair distance behind them. On the other side of the trees, several industrial warehouses grew closer and moments later the Jeep's wheels left the rough between the trees before slamming over a sidewalk onto a busy public road. Seconds later Sam's eyes were drawn upward to the military helicopter that suddenly appeared over their heads.

"They have eyes in the sky, Alex!" Sam yelled, as if she wasn't already aware.

The Jeep swerved and snaked between the somewhat congested traffic. Up ahead civilian vehicles were coming to a standstill. With her reflexes now at optimum, Alex swerved across the single lane, cutting off an oncoming car before she drove the Jeep through the far less congested lanes of a gas station and onto a secondary road. Somehow she shook the pursuant military vehicles but, above their heads, the helicopter continued to hover. The road snaked through a small residential area before it forked around a traffic circle and eventually onto a bypass. With it being far less busy than the other road, it allowed them to gain speed, but likewise, it afforded the perfect opportunity for the helicopter to open fire at them. Their machine gun shot off a multitude of bullets, slamming next to them into the tarmac. Since the Jeep was without a roof it left Alex and Sam entirely exposed and vulnerable. Now flanked by concrete Jersey barriers on either side of the lane, they had nowhere to go but forward. Another series of bullets ripped holes into the tarmac and bounced off the concrete lane dividers. Just ahead, only a few more yards of concrete barriers remained before the lane would be free for her to veer the vehicle off and under an overpass. But the helicopter was on top of them and they were now an easy target. In a pressured moment Alex pushed both feet down onto the brake sending clouds of blue smoke from the wheels into the air. The tires screeched as the vehicle came to a sudden halt. Above them, the large helicopter whipped forward over their heads, its size preventing it from carrying out any sudden maneuvers in response.

When it eventually managed to turn around, Alex had had sufficient time to speed up and continue forward along the bypass. Aiming for the end of the barriers it was a risky move, but in that moment under fire, had been her only option, and it paid off. They had gained enough time and distance that made their escape through the small clearing entirely possible. Yet, they remained fixed on the helicopter which headed toward them from the front, its nose and machine gun pointed directly at them. Utterly focused and keeping her wits about her, it was a game of chicken as the distance shortened between them and the fast approaching helicopter. Foreseeing their plan, the helicopter didn't waste another second and fired off the first round of bullets that successfully pierced the Jeep's grill before it hit the hood next and then smashed through the windscreen. Sam fired a single shot into the helicopter's gas tank when it swept over their heads, already preparing to turn around.

"Are you hit?" Sam yelled, while his eyes skimmed over her body for blood.

Alex didn't answer. Instead she pushed the Jeep forward until she reached the gap between the dividers and turned off into the oncoming lane. Clouds of black smoke billowed from the grill and escaped through the bullet holes in the hood, making it nearly impossible to see clearly. Behind them the helicopter had turned, relentless in its pursuit. Narrowly missing an oncoming bus, the Jeep reached the shelter of the overpass, and not a moment too soon as the engine cut out and burst into flames. Forced out of the vehicle Alex and Sam set off on foot. Using the overhanging road to conceal their location, their feet thumped down hard onto the road, navigating over sidewalks and between a multitude of motor-bikes until they reached the safety of a bustling shopping district. Out of breath, and in fear of being pursued, they kept running, weaving their way through the busy streets. They had no idea where they were or even where they were heading, but they kept running. Beads of sweat ran down their faces as the heat and extreme humidity beat down on their bodies. Looking back once only, they were fairly certain they weren't being followed anymore but they continued pushing through the hordes of pedestrians. They could no longer hear the helicopter above their heads. Up ahead, on the opposite side of the road, a welcoming shopping center beckoned and they spared no time in changing direction towards it.

Once inside they finally stopped running, taking shelter in one of the narrow passages that ran between two shops. Bent at the waist, with his hands resting on his knees, Sam breathed heavily in an effort to catch his breath. Likewise, with her eyes closed, Alex slid her back down against the wall and dropped exhausted into a squat. When they finally caught their breath, Alex spoke for the first time since they'd fled from the airfield.

"Chen deliberately led us into an ambush. That's why he was so cocky."

"Well, whatever he said or did, Jin Mu had his own score to settle with the guy and I doubt Chen saw that one coming either."

"We're going to need to find someplace safe to stay for the night, Sam. I have no idea what's going on and why we're the ones being hunted down, but one thing I do know, the manna is at the very center of it all."

"You're right. We need time to figure it out. It's out there somewhere and whoever has it, is under serious threat. A hundred thousand US dollars isn't small change," Sam noted. "So much for our honeymoon," he added as he helped her up.

"Adventure is the spice of life, Sam. We'll pick up where we left off once this is all done, promise. For now we just need to make sure we stay alive."

CHAPTER SEVENTEEN

The map bought from a nearby street vendor who conned tourists into signing up for cheap tours, told them they were in a small town about an hour outside of the city of Hong Kong. It was late afternoon and they were tired, hot and hungry. They aimlessly wandered up and down the side streets in search of a place to settle in for the night. Bar a few badly translated A-frame business billboards that stood along the pavements, everything—as expected—was written in Chinese. As they turned the corner into yet another side street, Sam spotted the bright red signage on the front of a building. It simply said *Rooms*. Relieved, they hurried toward it. Once inside it was as if a local textile factory had had a flash sale on their red velvet fabric. Every conceivable space, from the carpet to the small sofa, the drapes and everywhere in between, was covered with blood red velvet. When a short, fat, greasy Chinese man walked past them, hand in hand with a scantily clad girl, and up the stairs, it was quite evident what the nature of the establishment was. Alex hesitated and tugged Sam away from the front desk.

"It's a brothel, Sam. We can't stay here," she said in disgust.

"I don't think we have much choice at this stage, Alex. Besides, it's the one place no one will come looking for us. One night, just so we can rest and plan where to go from here, okay?"

A skinny, pale looking, elderly man sat behind the check-in desk. Wearing a dirty, white, sleeveless vest, and long black trousers he squinted his small eyes, that practically lay buried between his heavy eyelids and thick undereye bags. Next to him his cigarette smoldered in a cheap gold ashtray that hadn't been cleaned in centuries. Sam didn't flinch. Instead he slid an American fifty-dollar bill across the dusty counter. The man's eyes moved between Alex and Sam before he picked up the note and handed them a key from beneath the counter. Sam led Alex up the red velvet stairs which creaked noisily beneath their feet. Another working woman passed them on her way down the stairs, flirting unashamedly with Sam.

"I'll never understand it," Alex mumbled, once they passed her and reached the top of the stairs.

Trying hard not to take in the salacious sound effects along the way, the gold painted numbers on the wall pointed them to the end of the corridor where they found their room. Much like the red velvet decor downstairs, their room had undergone the same exaggerated furnishing in a sickly bile green. Stale cigarette smoke lay thick in the air, further escaping from beneath their feet with each step they took across the stained, greenish-brown carpet.

"I think I'm going to be sick," Alex muttered.

"If you are I'm sure it will blend in nicely," Sam giggled while he moved toward the only window in the room. He pushed the dusty drapes away to reveal an even filthier timber sash window that looked out onto the neighboring building's wall. When he eventually managed to force the window open—it was clear no one had opened it in years—the humid, pollution-filled air that pushed up between the tightly packed buildings brought little to no relief.

"I'll sleep standing up, thank you," Alex declared when she folded back the slippery green nylon bedspread to reveal a matching heavily stained sheet.

"You don't even want to see the bathroom," Sam commented when he exited the restroom covering his mouth and nose with the inside of his T-shirt. It's a dump, you're right. We might pick up something else but we certainly won't get any rest here."

Without another thought the two dashed out of the room, down the red velvet stairs and out into the street where, a mix of tension and exhaustion had them hysterically burst into laughter.

"How about we just get something to eat for now and then we find a bus to nowhere to catch up on a few hours of sleep afterwards?" Sam suggested.

"Deal," Alex said, still giggling as they walked off in search of a food market.

It didn't take them long to search one out as they soon found themselves immersed between countless tightly-squeezed food vendors all fighting to make their day's living. Heading into peak evening hours, women were frantically cooking and frying up anything that crawled the earth. Skewers of deep-fried scorpions, cockroaches, rats and spiders interspersed among dishes of noodles, fish and goat stews were on offer everywhere. The smells were oddly quite inviting, but the idea of eating a deep-fried locust held zero appeal to either of them. Following the narrow walkways between the vendors in search of food that offered more palatable westernized options, it soon became very crowded and Alex and Sam found themselves pushed through the market in a current of rushed locals. When they were finally ejected and deposited at the opposite end of the open market, they kept walking for fear of being pushed back in.

"That was quite the experience," Sam said, slightly out of breath, "I mean what would it take to get a simple hotdog around here?"

"Oh you'll get your dog, all right," Alex laughed before pointing to a nearby street café that seemed distinctly higher in class. For one thing they had a handful of two-seater tables and served mostly vegetables and noodle dishes. It was a safe option, they thought. The crease-free green and white checkered tablecloths were clean and looked far more inviting when they finally sat down at one of the small tables inside the semi-open café. It was also far less crowded with only a small number of patrons scattered between the eight small tables surrounding them. A friendly young male dressed in a crisp white apron, appeared out of nowhere and, pen and pad in hand, took position next to them. When he realized they were foreigners, he promptly switched to English, all the while smiling from ear to ear.

"How may I serve you tonight?" the friendly waiter asked in near perfect English.

"Oh, great, you speak English," Alex said with a sigh of relief.

"Most of the younger generation do these days, yes. Would you like me to suggest something off our menu?"

"Tell you what, yes, surprise us, as long as the dishes don't contain any kind of animal or its internal parts," Sam said after which the bubbly waiter promptly disappeared behind a curtain into the small kitchen.

Alex sank down into the chair and pushed her hands into the pockets of her pants, settling into a more comfortable position to rest. Instantly her back stiffened as she sat upright again and dug one hand deeper inside her pocket.

"What? What's wrong?" Sam asked when her sudden movements alarmed him.

She didn't answer. Instead she pulled her fisted hand from her pocket and dropped the crumpled blue piece of fabric in the middle of the table.

"I forgot I had this," she declared before her eyes started searching through the multitude of bright signs up and down the street behind them.

"If it is a company logo I strongly doubt you'll find it here, Alex. I reckon we'd have a better chance of tracking it down in Hong Kong. According to the map it's about ninety minutes by train from here."

Alex relaxed her back again but continued to rub the fabric between her fingers.

"You're right. We should find a train. If nothing else, at least it would give us a chance to rest for the duration of the trip."

"Do you work there?" The effervescent waiter's voice startled her as he popped two plates of Chow Mein on the table in front of them.

"Where?" Alex asked, confused with his question.

"There, at Infinitech." He pointed his chin towards the fabric in her hand as he pulled their chopsticks and a bottle of soy sauce from his apron's pocket.

Alex straightened into an upright position again, stretching the fabric out between her fingers in search of the name.

"My sister works there. She was lucky enough to get accepted this year. My father is very proud of her. You won't believe how quickly those fifty positions fill up each year. She says it looks better on the inside than in the magazines," the chatty waiter continued.

"You know this place?" Sam queried, now also paying keen attention.

"Yes, of course. Who doesn't?" he said, instantly realizing they obviously didn't.

"At least here in China everyone knows Infinitech," he quickly added, smoothing out the tablecloth.

"Where are they?" Alex asked.

"On Bio Island of course. Can I bring you some drinks?"

"And where's that?" Sam asked ignoring his offer for something to drink.

"You don't know where Bio Island is? Wow, where are you from? Africa?"

"England actually, and no, we don't often hear much about China's industries over there," Sam answered him with an amused expression.

"So how do we find this island?" Alex interrupted.

"It's not an island, well actually it is, sort of. It's in Guangzhou. You can catch the intercity train from here to Shenzhen and then the high-speed train will take you straight there. It's about three hours total. Drinks?" He tried again.

"So you say it's called Infinitech. What do they do?" Alex cut in again.

"They're the largest biotech firm in the world."

The waiter leaned in and proceeded to whisper behind his hand. "My sister says she heard they're about to make a major breakthrough. But don't tell anyone I told you. She could get fired."

"Oh, of course, thank you. And yes, you may bring us those

drinks please?" Sam said cheerily as he tucked into his bowl of noodles.

"Biotech? Why would a biotechnology company hire a Chinese street gang to find the manna and go as far as commit murder for it? What could they possibly want to do with it that's so important?" Alex asked as her brain started working through the millions of questions that flooded her mind.

"I don't know, but this Chow Mein is the best I've ever had."

"Focus, Sam! We just found out that a biotechnology company is behind the manna's disappearance, not to mention the fact that they're trying to kill us and that they might have also killed the priest, and all you can think about is food!"

Sam paused, stuffing another mouthful of noodles into his mouth first before he spoke.

"Calm down, Alex. We don't know if they're the ones behind the theft nor that they killed the priest. All this fabric proves is that a Fang member wore a piece of clothing with their badge on it. It's entirely possible one of the gang members stole the piece of clothing in the first place. It doesn't mean he's actually working there or was hired by them. Nevertheless, you're right. We will go there and check them out ourselves. I agree, none of this makes any sense. But I do know you need to eat and rest. We'll catch the next train out and be there in the morning."

It wasn't what Alex wanted to hear, but she conceded. They'd gone twenty-four hours straight without food or sleep and that's what they both needed now more than anything. That, and to stay alive. She stuffed the patch of fabric back into her pocket and lifted a helping of noodles into her mouth just as the chatty waiter popped two bottles of aloe infused soft drinks in front of them. Next to them, he placed a blue and white brochure on the table between them along with the bill.

"What's this?" Alex asked as Sam paid the waiter.

"Your golden ticket," the waiter joked before he added, "hope to see you again here soon."

And just like that, he bounced over to the next table to take their order.

CHAPTER EIGHTEEN

The 'golden ticket' turned out to be an exclusive invitation for a private VIP tour of Bio Island, clearly given to their generous waiter by his sister. Now, with a clear direction in mind, they had no trouble hopping onto a tram that took them to the nearest intercity station, after which, with only a short wait for the next underground speed train, they soon found themselves heading northbound from Shenzhen directly to Bio Island.

"One thing about China is that it never sleeps. Where are all these people going this late at night?" Alex tried making conversation with Sam who had already propped his jacket under his head.

"Home to go to sleep, which is what you should be doing now too," he said wryly as he closed his eyes.

But no matter how hard Alex tried, she simply couldn't sleep. Her head was tirelessly working through the events that had now brought them to the middle of China. Her mind trailed back to the look in Stavros' eyes when he received the news of his mother's death, and the utter disappointment at failing her that was written all over his face. She thought of Khalil's daughters and how he had risked everything for them only to almost lose his life to help them find the truth. The frazzled images of the three priests back at the church in Bari was the last thought she had before she must have drifted off into a deep slumber that had her sleep through all four train stops en route. It was only when Sam planted a gentle kiss on her forehead that she woke up.

"We're here, sunshine," he whispered as he slipped his arms into the sleeves of his tan leather jacket. "Glad you got at least a few hours' sleep. We all know how grumpy you get when you don't rest," he joked.

Still waking up from her deep slumber, Alex smiled at how well Sam knew her.

It was well past midnight when they stepped off onto the high-tech platform on Bio Island. It didn't look anything like any of the subway stations they were used to. Instead, it looked like the inside of a spaceship; all silver and shiny with bright lights and modern features. Aside from Alex and Sam, there were only a half dozen security guards who also stepped off the train and it didn't take much to figure out they were quite obviously making their way in to work to report for their graveyard shift duties. The air was much clearer than the congested, polluted air in the inner city and the much cooler night temperature brought a welcome relief from the sweltering humidity of the day. Their eyes followed the group of chatty, red-uniformed guards moving in unison down towards the lower end of the sleek narrow walkway. Keeping their distance they decided to follow them, surmising that they'd probably be heading to another mode of transportation. They were right. Just on the other side of an enormous digital billboard that displayed an aerial image of the entire island, a row of Segways neatly lined an impressively clean brick colored concrete track.

They waited for the guards to leave, pretending to study the brochure in Alex's hand. Behind the billboard that stood bolted to the ground, at least fifteen feet high and double that in width, a red square indicated the position where they were now on top of a bright green image that resembled the outlines of a leaf, and next to them, the flashing lights of a bright blue 3D globe. The chatty waiter had been correct when he'd said it was an island of sorts and Alex and Sam found themselves backing away from the billboard to take it all in.

"I've never seen anything like it," Sam said. "It's actually an island in the middle of China."

"Well technically it's between two branches of the Pearl River in the south-east of China." Alex said smartly, eliciting a sideways glance from Sam.

"What? I'm just saying. It's what it says here on the brochure," Alex giggled as she continued through the waiter's parting gift.

"What else does it say on there, hotshot?"

"Well, it's part of about four hundred and fifty acres of development that's known as the Guangzhou Development

District and Bio Island is in fact a group of biotechnology companies housed smack bang in the middle of it."

"So that's what this flashing globe is, then," Sam said. "So what are we waiting for? Let's get on with it."

"It's two o'clock in the morning, Sam. The tour doesn't start until 8 a.m. Besides, if you haven't noticed it yet, we're being watched. If we hover around outside the building it will, without doubt, raise a few alarm bells."

Sam's eyes caught sight of more than a handful security cameras that were cleverly camouflaged as lamp posts; spaced every couple of yards apart along the treelined Segway track. He swiftly turned his gaze back to the billboard.

"Your eagle eyes miss nothing. Well spotted." Sam stared at the polarized dot on the digital display board before adding. "Well we can't stay here either, and as far as I can tell, there aren't any luxurious beach hotels on this island."

"There has to be a blind spot between the cameras some-where," Alex said.

"Or hopefully an exhausted guard at the end of his shift," Sam joked, then asked, not expecting an answer, "Shall we see if perhaps we can escape the paparazzi and find a bench or something until morning?"

Their two-wheeled motorized vehicles' wheels whirred noisily across the brick colored track in the quiet of the night. There wasn't a leaf that moved nor signs of any life beyond their own. Above their heads the security cameras continued to line the pathway as they followed their every movement towards the towering building that stood glowing in the darkness. It was only as they drew nearer to the high-tech structure that a full appreciation of the building could be gained. Stretching at least forty stories high into the sky, it looked like the cornerstone of a giant fortress. Shaped in a perfect square, it was entirely made of glass on all four sides, the edges of which were illuminated by bright blue globes that lit the structure up like a Christmas tree.

In the distance up ahead, the faint sound of voices forced their attention back to the risks at hand. Two security guards were on patrol and walking towards them. Relieved they hadn't been noticed yet, Alex and Sam veered off the path between the trees and across a wide-open grassed area. Their mode of transportation proved to be challenging as the wheels slipped across the turf. It was only when they jumped off their Segways that they realized the lack of tire grip was because of it being artificial grass.

"It's too noisy anyway," Sam whispered as they lowered the two-wheelers flush with the ground.

Their eyes frantically searched for a hiding place, welcoming the fact that at least they were somewhat sheltered in the darkness. But there was none. The entire building was surrounded by open stretches of imitation grass, and apart from the few trees that lined the pathway, they were now entirely exposed. Deciding their best option was to lie face down on the ground and wait it out, they moved, hunched down, as far away from where they had left their two-wheelers as they could, and lay down on the turf. Unable to move and look up, they perceived the two guards suddenly fall silent. The men remained, paused in the silence, for what seemed like an eternity. Alex pinched her eyes shut as if she was wishing them away, pushing her face as far down into the fake grass as was possible. If they got caught now there'd be zero chance of them ever getting inside Infinitech to find the manna. But when they heard the abrupt Chinese commands echo towards them, they instantly knew they had been discovered. Barely audible, Sam cursed into the artificial grass that irritatingly pressed into his mouth. But they still didn't move. Partly because they knew they had run out of options and partly because they couldn't see if the guards were aiming any weapons at them. The latter uncertainty was soon to be cleared up when, mere seconds later, the two guards stood directly over them and Alex and Sam heard the familiar sound of the hammers on their revolvers pull back as bullets were loaded into the firing chambers.

Having no option but to surrender, Alex and Sam stretched their hands out above their heads while slowly raising their heads, spitting a few blades of grass out as they did so. Two uniformed guards nervously hovered over them, continually shouting abrupt commands at them in Chinese.

"English, we don't understand you," Sam said, and a brief moment later, one of them simply yelled a single word in English back at them.

"Up!"

"Okay, okay, take it easy," Sam said as they slowly rose to their feet.

Now upright, Sam's sheer height, more than a foot taller than either guard, immediately sent them into sheer panic. It was quite evident that it was the most action they'd found themselves in, quite possibly ever. When Sam could no longer hide his amusement, he glanced at Alex sideways. He was right, she thought. They could so easily take down these two inexperienced guards, but what good would that do? She now realized that this unplanned incident might very well provide the perfect access into Infinitech long before the tour even started.

When Alex didn't make any effort to escape, Sam was quick to catch on to her genius plan. They'd play along and use it to their advantage. Once inside, they'd figure out a way to escape, after they'd found the manna. So when the shortest of the two guards nervously instructed his colleague to cuff Sam while he took on Alex—he had the slightly bigger physique between the two—Sam didn't resist. The relief on the guard's face instantly showed and it took everything for Sam and Alex not to explode into laughter.

As they were ushered back onto the pale red concrete path, the guard's sweaty palms tightened around Sam's wrists and it promptly occurred to him that the guards had never searched them for weapons. Behind him the guard still puffed heavily in the wake of the adrenaline-charged event that had disturbed their routine night patrol and, as the sudden surge of stress slowly disappeared from his body, he finally found the courage to speak to his colleague again—no doubt comparing notes or possibly to check if they had followed the correct protocol. They brought their trespassers to a halt in front of the seamless glass door at the front of the tall building. The short one barked a sudden command at his partner before he pushed Alex closer to Sam handing her into his partner's custody. Alex and Sam patiently watched as the guard moved his body one glass panel to the left and stared directly at his own image where it reflected back at him through the mirrored pane. An instant later, a thin green horizontal line moved over his body before he was prompted to press his left palm against the glass. The green outline of his hand flashed back before the glass door in front of Alex and Sam receded and silently slid sideways.

CHAPTER NINETEEN

B ehind them the glass door promptly moved back into place as if there had never been a door there at all. It was as if they had stepped into a brightly illuminated alien ship of some kind. Beneath their feet the shiny, white floor squeaked under the guards' shoes as they nudged their prisoners forward into the expansive entrance. From the inside, the glass windows had now transformed into stark white walls which surrounded them entirely. There was no ceiling above their heads. Instead, an open shaft escaped high up into space between floor upon floor that surrounded the atrium's outer edges. As they were ushered toward a pair of matching stark white capsules positioned on the furthest end of the massive space, a three-dimensional image of a friendly Chinese hostess erupted from the floor in front of them. Startled by the hologram, Sam unintentionally broke free from the guard's grip as he sidestepped the coherent light source, sending the guard into a sudden flare of panic.

"It's all good, mate. Just got a fright," Sam said calmly and allowed the frazzled guard to wrap his sweaty palms around his arms again. Along the walls several glass panes had been replaced by digital screens upon which silent images of a red and white helix, happy children playing on a playground, and a contrasting funeral scene rotated in random sequence before it ended with the bright red Infinitech logo.

When they reached the enormous twin pods the shorter guard placed his palm on the capsule wall after which the bottom three-quarters of the pod receded into the floor while the top remained hovering in the air.

"Get!" the guard barked at Alex and Sam, prompting them to move forward under the pod umbrella before they stepped in with them. As suddenly as the pod's wall receded it advanced back into position, closing them inside the pod. A short command left the guard's mouth and Alex and Sam felt what they had now determined was in fact an elevator, descend below the building. When the elevator pod opened after just a few seconds, they stepped out into a shiny stain-less-steel corridor that appeared as sterile as the area they had just left, except it was far less inviting. Instead of the shiny white floor their feet now moved over a gridded metal floor and, to Sam, it felt as if the steel walls and ceiling were closing in on him. It was as if they were walking upright through a ventilation duct. Sam nervously looked sideways at Alex who seemed as on edge as he did. When they reached the end of the long 'duct' Alex and Sam were somewhat pleasantly surprised to be stopped by a far more ordinary looking metal door. Again, as with the last two doorways they had passed through, the guard's hand unlocked the door and they felt themselves being shoved inside a small windowless steel room before the guards disappeared and the door locked behind them.

"What is this place?" Alex finally spoke.

"Quite something, isn't it? I've heard China had mind-blowing technology, but this is on an entirely different level."

"Their computer technology might be mind-blowing but their security needs work," Alex announced as she pulled a hairpin from her back pocket and promptly set about unlocking her handcuffs before freeing Sam from his. Alone in the steel box they each traced their eyes along the solid steel walls in search of a camera or microphone before, having found none, settling on the floor against one of the walls.

"How many floors below ground do you think we are?" Alex asked Sam.

"Who knows how fast that weird capsule elevator goes. Your guess is as good as mine."

Alex glanced at her watch. "Well, we have a few hours until sunrise. My guess is they'll wait until morning before they report us."

"The way I see it, we have two choices," Sam said with a twinkle in his eyes.

"Oh, I know that look Sam Quinn. Handcuffs I can get out of. An electronic door, not so much."

"We should at least try, right?" Sam was already on his feet inspecting the door. His hands glided along the narrow outlines of the door. There was no door handle, digital pad or anything similar. He placed his ear against the steel panel but heard nothing and then tried pushing his body against it.

"Told you," Alex mocked as she let her head drop back against the wall behind her and continued to watch Sam's hands move over every inch of the door. Yet, it yielded nothing. He stood back from the door and placed his hands on his hips staring at the door.

"There has to be a way to open this door," he expressed in frustration.

"There isn't, Sam. At least not without the guy's hand. We should get some sleep. If nothing else this place is clean enough to eat off the floors."

Sam had just about turned to follow her advice when he blurted out, "That's it! The guy's hand!"

He crossed to the opposite pane. "It was his left hand, wasn't it?"

"Yes, why?"

But Sam didn't answer. Instead his knuckles eagerly rapped the approximate area on the steel panel where the guard had placed his hand to unlock the door while he pressed his left ear flush against the panel.

"What are you...?"

"Shh!" he flung back at Alex and continued to knock against the panel.

When the hollow echoes subsided and instead a solid dull thump reverberated from behind where his knuckles hit the steel, he stopped.

"Got it!"

"Got what?" Alex asked, rising to join him at the door.

"The digital box. It's here." Sam had placed his palm flat against the panel, his fingers fanned.

"It won't open without the security guy's palmprint, Sam."

"How soundproof do you think it is in here?" Sam asked an arbitrary question ignoring her skepticism.

"No idea. Why does that even matter right now?" Alex said confused as she carefully surveyed Sam's face. It was very evident his mind had gone off on its own mission.

"Stand back," Sam ordered and pulled his gun from under his jacket before aiming it directly at the invisible digital box hidden behind the metal wall.

He fired a single shot into the wall long before Alex had made sense of his plan. A few sparks burst from the bullet hole in the wall as Sam waited for the door to open. But it didn't. He instantly fired off another bullet which caused a much bigger set of flashing lights produced by the sudden disruptive electrical charge. The door clicked and sprang away from the surrounding walls.

"Are you staying or coming with?" Sam mocked as Alex stood mesmerized by his successful breakout; she simply smiled with admiration.

The duct-like corridor was undisturbed when they popped their heads around the doorway before they stealthily moved along the gridded steel floor. When they reached the very spot where the capsuled elevator had spat them out, there was nothing but a clear steel shaft in its place. A low railing surrounded the inside of the shaft behind which there was nothing but darkness. Peering up into the dark shaft the underbelly of the capsuled pod was barely visible roughly fifty feet above them. They stepped back scouring for another way out then Alex, staring down the long passage that continued beyond their holding cell suggested, "Let's go that way."

Their feet thumped on the lattice steel squares as they hurried down the corridor, passing the room they had just escaped from before the passage suddenly turned ninety degrees to the right. They had just turned the corner when the short hallway suddenly stopped at the bottom of a spiral steel staircase. Taking caution Sam looked up but, unable to see beyond the darkness, quickly started ascending the stairs with Alex closely behind him.

With their guns held in position, they quietly made their way up the multitude of steel steps, estimating that they had long since passed the fifty-foot mark. When it finally stopped at a small landing that opened up into a stark white corridor, it had become apparent that they must have reached one of the floors that extended above the capsule elevator in the main entrance.

"Wait!" Alex called out to Sam as he moved to exit the landing.

"There's a camera," she whispered, pointing to its position directly above the small doorway. The flashing red light indicated it was on. With their backs against the inside walls on either side of the entrance into the passage they each surveyed along the length of the white corridor.

"Clear," Alex whispered to which Sam echoed the same. They fixed their eyes on the small camera above their heads as it slowly swiveled away from the end of the passage.

"Now," Sam signaled before they stepped out and swiftly moved down the sterile corridor away from the camera's view.

Alex paused when the wall suddenly gave way to the large window to a laboratory. Inside several cages of white mice lined the surface of a long stainless-steel table. Her eyes settled on one particular cage that bore the mutilated bodies of three dead mice. It repulsed her, realizing they had been the unfortunate subjects of a bad experiment.

"This way." Sam urged her towards a cloakroom when he caught sight of the camera that was slowly making its way back to them. And not a moment too soon.

Safely out of sight from the camera's eye, they slipped into a changing room. Rows of red lockers stretched down the center of the room, mirrored by several more that lined the walls on both sides. The striking sound of a locker door closing came from somewhere in the back of the locker room before they heard footsteps moving towards them. Unable to retreat back into the range of the camera's lens in the passage they froze. Staring down the two aisles on either side of the row of lockers along the center of the room, ears strained in an effort to distinguish the imminent approaching footsteps, they waited in silence. Allowing her instincts to direct her, Alex pulled Sam toward the left aisle where they each turned and paused in front of a locker. Now, only separated by the back to back row of lockers between them, they anxiously listened as the footsteps moved along the floor and disappeared into the hallway. Relieved she had trusted her intuition, Alex continued further into the room in search of any more unexpected employees, and soon discovered they were alone. At the end of the rows of lockers Sam spotted a container and lifted its lid to reveal a pile of worn lab coats. He reached in and pulled out two coats which they promptly slipped on. Alex found herself staring at the embroidered red logo on Sam's chest, pulled out the patch of fabric from her pocket and flattened it against the image. There was no mistaking it. Infinitech was indeed behind their attacks.

CHAPTER TWENTY

C amouflaged in their stolen white lab coats they quietly set off through the facility in search of answers. They passed several research rooms that were thankfully unoccupied as a result of it being outside normal working hours. Alex took note of the surveillance cameras that were strategically placed along the corridors, as they made every effort to play the part of Infinitech employees. When the nearest camera's angle changed it afforded Alex the brief opportunity to tug on a laboratory's door in the hope that it would open, but it didn't. So they continued on and, after trying several more doors with no success Alex started getting anxious. Walking aimlessly up and down the corridors was not helping their disguise or getting them any nearer to finding the answers they sought.

"We need to find a way off this floor, Sam. We've been walking up and down these white halls for some time now and sooner or later an overzealous guard monitoring these cameras will catch on and come for us. There has to be an elevator or stairs to another floor here somewhere."

"I agree, but all I see are unoccupied research labs and by my reckoning it won't be long before real employees start arriving for work or someone discovers that we escaped from our underground prison. The best we can do right now is to keep moving."

Passing yet another locked research room, Sam snatched a clipboard from where it hung on a hook attached to the door. Using it as a prop in order to pass one more CCTV camera they turned down the next empty corridor. Relief washed over them when they stumbled upon an elevator.

"Bingo!" Sam exclaimed; although his excitement was possibly more due to the fact that the elevator had ordinary buttons to press and didn't require any complicated hand-print identification.

"Up or down?" he asked, knowing Alex's intuition was worth more than a haphazard guess at this point.

"Up," she answered quickly.

When the white elevator doors closed them inside, the silence soon broke into a high-pitched nasal vocalist whose traditional Chinese song accompanied them all the way to the forty-second floor. The elevator took less than sixty seconds before the doors opened and they found themselves staring into a sizable office that stretched out in front of them.

"So this must be the boss's office," Sam commented when the pair stepped out onto the luxurious bamboo crafted floor and they gazed out across the entire Bio Island through the three-hundred-and=sixty-degree floor to ceiling windows that wrapped around the elevator situated in the middle of the room.

"This is what I call a corner office," Sam added, still mesmerized by the grandeur of it all.

"We don't have a lot of time, Sam. We need to find the manna and whatever proof we can lay our hands on that points to the priest's murder."

Alex had already yanked open the narrow drawer that stretched the length of the pristine desk that was magnificently crafted in shades of red, green and burnt umber which transmuted into black towards the flared legs that looked much like swords. When she found nothing but a letter opener and a newspaper written entirely in Chinese, she slammed the drawer shut and stared at the writhing dragon painted on the bare tabletop.

"There's nothing here. Not one single piece of paper or file that tells us who this company is and why they killed to get the manna."

Frustrated and at a loss what to do next they circled around the elevator through the large office that contained nothing but the single desk and a few chairs.

"We're missing something, Sam. Why have this enormous office with no furniture except an empty desk in one corner? There's not even a computer or a television screen. Nothing," Alex muttered.

"Maybe it's just that, an empty office. With a billion-dollar view, of course," Sam said.

But Alex wasn't convinced and she continued to pace across the bamboo floor. In a moment of frustration she threw her head back to stretch out a knot in her neck and caught a glimpse of an oddly shaped circular panel in the ceiling above her head. She paused and stared at the inconsistency between the otherwise square roof panels that surrounded it.

"That's odd."

"What?" Sam asked, then stood gazing up at the spot she had pointed out.

They were standing in the middle of the large empty space on the other side of the elevator.

"If I didn't know better I'd expect water to rain down from it. It almost looks like one of those ostentatious showers," Alex said as she tried to solve the puzzling anomaly above their heads.

Sam waved his hands above his head as if he was flagging down a taxi.

"What are you doing?" Alex giggled.

"Trying to activate the sensors, but nothing's happening. If it were a shower we'd both be drenched by now."

"I don't think it's a shower. It's something else. We need to look for a button or a remote," Alex ventured.

Alex found herself back at the desk, gliding her hands across the surface and underneath the scrolling apron that ran around the desk's top. When she found nothing she smoothed her hands down all four of the sword-like legs.

"Nothing here," she reported, while Sam's hands searched the paneling around the elevator.

Alex stood back and inspected the desk from every angle before she found herself once again staring down at the ornately painted dragon, her eyes peering deep into the dragon's black eyes. Her hands rested, much like Father Guido's had back at the Basilica di Nichola, as she remained fixed on its eyes. Something about it seemed strange and she traced her fingers over the two black circles. Instantly they turned a glowing red beneath her fingers, prompting her to snatch her hand to her chest fearing she might have triggered an alarm. Sam's voice bellowed from behind the elevator, summoning Alex to join him. She found him staring at a digital laser display that had appeared from the odd shaped panel in the ceiling and projected through almost the entire space. The hologram ran from the ceiling to the floor and was visible from any direction. They stood in awe, watching the screen share several images of lab technicians at work while a honey-toned female voice shared an introduction to Infinitech in perfect English. Enthralled by the sophisticated private audio-visual tour on display in front of them they took it all in, hypnotized by its high-tech delivery.

"I would have given you a private tour if only you asked," a gentle voice spoke behind them.

Startled Alex and Sam spun around and stared down the barrels of four burly men's handguns. Between them stood the man with the gentle voice, his pitch-black hair slicked back into a prominent side part. When Alex's hand reached for her gun behind her back the man's entourage moved forward in unison, aiming their guns directly at their faces. Forced to surrender their weapons, Alex and Sam handed them to the four bodyguards.

"You're not going to get away with this," Alex challenged the man.

"And what exactly would *this* be?" the man asked. "You broke into my office," he added.

"You killed the priest and stole the manna. Not to mention that you placed a bounty on our heads."

Alex noticed the subtle nuances of surprise on the man's face. "Yes, we know it was you," she persisted.

The man didn't answer and she proceeded to push for a confession.

"What I fail to understand is why. Why would a company like yours want the manna when it can heal so many people?"

Sam, who had stood quietly watching, allowing Alex to interrogate the man, suddenly spoke.

"You manufacture regenerative medicine, isn't it? You want to use it. That's the breakthrough you're currently working on." Sam was elated when he realized he had figured it out.

"How do you know about that?" the man said with surprise.

"There's a lot we know," Alex diverted his question when she recalled the waiter pleading for them not to divulge his sister's scoop.

The man smiled and beckoned toward his men to turn them around to face the hologram. He retrieved a small remote from his luxurious silk suit's jacket pocket and clicked it with his thumb.

"Allow me to give you the full tour, Sam and Alex Quinn," he said, pausing for effect as he allowed them to register that he knew exactly who they were. When their faces displayed the reaction he desired, he drew their attention back to the formal presentation of digital imagery that beamed across the room.

"My name is Dr. Shuren Wang and Infinitech Group is the result of my life's work as a biotechnologist. Contrary to what you assumed, our sole purpose here at Infinitech is to save lives. We're not in the business of killing people, of which you so vehemently accused me. We build new life, create cures, restore longevity, prevent death. As Sam so aptly pointed out, we spend billions each year on creating regenerative pharmaceuticals that will one day cure cancer, dementia, Alzheimer's, you name it. We've given thousands of people around the world hope, when they had none left. Our medicines restored their health and added years to their lives, to spend with their loved ones, when previously they had mere days or weeks left to live and the world had failed them. Do you know how great it is to see a child happy when our stem cell transplant saves one of his siblings or when our nanotechnology destroys an inoperable brain tumor in one of his parents? You of all people should understand this, Dr. Quinn. Since when is creating life a crime?"

"When you kill innocent priests and inflict brutal beatings on ordinary citizens it is most definitely a crime," Alex hissed at him, not in the least surprised that he was aware of Sam's background.

Shuren Wang turned away from the hologram and faced Alex. "I did not kill or assault anyone."

"You stole the manna, Dr. Wang, that makes you the prime suspect in my book," Alex added as her weighted words struck a nerve with him that propelled him to take up a stance at the window.

"That's it, isn't it? The breakthrough. You needed the manna to complete whatever compound you're working on. That's why you wanted it so badly that you killed for it," Sam's voice cut across the space.

Wang spun around, his body rigid and his face fraught with anger.

"You're accusing me of a murder I did not commit. Yes, I went to meet with the church in Bari to negotiate a price for the manna. It was intended to be a legitimate offer, but sadly the priest wouldn't have it. The next thing we knew, he was dead."

"Which is precisely why you ordered the Fangs to bully us and the priests into finding it for you." Alex pushed back, but the expression on Wang's face was undeniable. He had no idea what she was talking about. Perplexed, Alex glanced at Sam who had noticed it too.

"I think we're done here," Wang said in an emotionless tone, after which he muttered an instruction to his men who promptly moved toward Alex and Sam and shoved them toward the elevator.

CHAPTER TWENTY-ONE

While they were being ushered to their holding cell somewhere on the thirty-third floor, they had both noticed that the entire floor had been unoccupied and it seemed none of the research labs were or had ever been in use. Much like the first room they'd been kept in by the security guards, Alex and Sam found themselves shoved into a roughly five by four foot sized room. But unlike the cold gray steel walls of their first dungeon-like underground lock-up, this one's walls were as stark white and clinical looking as the rest of the decor throughout the building. As soon as the door shut and locked behind them, they set about searching for a way out. Except for the two small ventilation ducts where the ceiling met two walls on opposite sides, there were no windows, yet the room seemed much colder than the rest of the building. Wasting no time, Sam followed the same routine of rapping his knuckles against the walls as he had done before, but this time, it didn't yield the same result. The walls were entirely solid all around. The thought had crossed their minds that the room was quite possibly intended as a cold storage which would have meant there'd be no way out of it even if they had their weapons.

"It's useless, Sam. This place is shut tight."

Sam moved away from the door and stretched his legs out next to where Alex had already sat down against one of the walls.

"He can't keep us here forever. Wang didn't strike me as a killer," Sam spoke.

"What makes you think that? This is his company after all and the patch of fabric came from one of these lab overcoats which was worn by one of Khalil's attackers. Not to mention that Wang said he had gone to Bari, hence admitting that he's after the manna for whatever breakthrough pharmaceutical they're working on. The dots line up, Sam. You can't argue with the facts."

"I hear you, and yes, the facts line up, but did you see his face when you told him about the Fangs? He had no idea. I don't know, Alex. I believe the man."

"Then why hold us at gunpoint and lock us up in here?"

"Because we broke into his office, Alex. And dare I remind you that we now also know what they're working on. We're a threat. Ever heard of corporate espionage? Rival companies would do and pay just about anything to sabotage their competitors' endeavors just to beat them to it. Specialist phar-maceuticals is an extremely competitive business. There's billions at stake with medical breakthroughs like this and if I know one thing it's that China has made serious advances in both biotech and space. They have the added advantage over other countries of having a lot of people and their strength lies in their numbers. I mean think about it. They've already successfully cloned monkeys. Imagine what would happen if they were successful at creating a pill that cures cancer or grows a brand-new human kidney?"

"So you think someone else is behind the priest's murder? A rival company. So this has nothing to do with the church, then?"

Sam shrugged his shoulders. "I'm not sure, but corporate cloak-and-dagger activities make a whole lot more sense, don't they?"

Alex pulled the piece of fabric from her pocket and rubbed it like one would a genie's lamp. The partial Chinese word below the logo still puzzled her. She traced her fingers over the raised red cotton. In her mind she was digesting Sam's theory and she couldn't deny that he might be right. It was entirely possible that they were caught in the middle of a corporate war. She stuck the fabric back in her pocket and rested her head on Sam's shoulder, closing her eyes for just a brief moment.

E xhausted from the past days' events, having not slept much, they must have both dozed off. It was only when Sam coughed and the motion of his shoulder tilted Alex's head forward that she started to come around. She tried to open her eyes but for some reason the message from her brain to her eyelids was delayed and it took more effort than usual. Her lungs felt tight as if she was coming down with the flu. She coughed in an attempt to clear her airways but instead it left a burning sensation in her lungs and in the back of her throat, laboring her breathing even further. Her body felt heavy and her limbs weak as she lifted her head. Sam coughed next to her again and she called out to him, not recognizing the slurred words that escaped from her mouth and which had no effect. She felt entirely out of control and unable to react to any of the messages flooding her brain. Panic rushed through her body, the adrenaline forcing her eyes open and she slowly became alert to the fact that they were both propped up against the wall like two puppets without their strings.

"Sam," she called out, sounding like a drunk again. Her lips were barely moving while her tongue lay thick against the roof of her mouth. Staring at her lap her vision was somewhat blurry. Sam called out her name next to her, sounding as drunk as she had. She knew they hadn't had any alcohol. She answered him by uttering a one syllable sound before the pressure on her lungs made her cough again. She reached out to touch his leg, having to work her arm and fingers hard to obtain any result. Sam lifted his head, mumbling something she couldn't quite make out, before his head flopped back against the wall. She clumsily pushed her thumb into his thigh again.

"Sam," she slurred, "wake up."

He groaned but opened his eyes. "I'm up, I'm up," he spoke in slow motion as he lifted his head and strained his eyes. He too felt heavy and drowsy.

"Why do I feel like we had too much to drink?" he moaned while lifting his hand to his eye but hitting his nose instead.

"I don't know but I feel very sleepy and my lungs hurt. Something's wrong Sam."

Alex pushed herself up off the floor, her legs feeling like that of a newborn foal when he tries to walk for the first time. She lost her balance and fell against the wall, praying desperately for the room to stop spinning. She looked back at Sam where he had stumbled to his feet in much the same way.

"Where's all this smoke coming from?" she asked waving her hand through a cloud of yellow haze, coughing profusely as she did so.

Sam's panicked voice behind her startled her. "It's not smoke, Alex. Cover your mouth and nose!" His words, although slightly less slurry, were muffled as he spoke from beneath his shirt where he had pulled the collar over half his face.

Alex did as he instructed, grateful for the immediate relief her T-shirt brought.

"It's a toxic gas," Sam announced as he pulled her towards the door and started banging his fists against it.

"Help! Let us out!" he yelled, his voice raspier and lower than usual.

Alex joined in while still fighting to rid her lungs from the sharp stinging that seemed to have gotten stuck somewhere in her throat now too.

But their lethargic efforts proved futile and instead, only

exacerbated the urgent need for fresh air in their lungs. The haze had become thicker and made it even harder to breathe in, even with the added barrier of cotton from their shirts. Alex felt her legs weaken beneath her as her body fought harder against the gas that was getting thicker by the second. Her fists slammed against the door next to Sam's whose strength appeared to have also evaporated now. Once again the room reeled and her vision went blurry. She was aware of Sam's hand around her arm and a loud siren that pierced her eardrums. But then everything went black and she no longer had any control over her body as her legs gave way and she slumped to the floor.

"**A**lex, can you hear me?"

The male voice sounded distant when Alex finally managed to open her eyes. She tried to speak but something was obstructing her mouth. Her throat was on fire, so too were her lungs. She tried to move her feet but couldn't. Her body felt like lead. Above her head a bright light slowly came into vision and she became cognizant of a whooshing sound somewhere to her left. She tried to turn her head to see what it was but again her body wasn't responding. In her mind she was anxious and afraid and yet her body experienced complete tranquility, as if it had somehow been removed from her head and existed on its own. The male voice spoke again.

"You're okay, just breathe slowly. You're on a ventilator."

Dr. Wang's sleek black hair with the prominent side part was slightly blurry before it slowly came into focus and she could see his eyes suddenly hover over her face. Somewhere in her muddled thoughts she realized in that instant that Sam was right. Those weren't the eyes of a killer. Across his nose and mouth a semi-transparent mask muffled his words. She tried to communicate her thoughts with her eyes hoping he'd tell her what she needed to know. It worked and his gentle voice spoke from beneath the mask again.

"Sam's okay. He's in the bed next to you. You're both fine. You're in the Infinitech infirmary. We were forced to place you under quarantine but we're taking good care of you. We're not quite sure what happened but it appears someone tried to poison you with a toxic nerve gas. My security managed to get you out just in time. You need to rest. The doctors say you'll recover completely and that sensation to your body should be restored within the next twelve hours. I have the best doctors on duty and I've ordered my men to keep guard and keep you both safe. All you need to do is rest."

Another masked figure pushed Wang to one side. Alex followed him with her eyes, aware he was fiddling with something that was just outside her vision. She wanted to get up and go check on Sam, but no matter how hard she tried, her body did not respond at all. A tear escaped her eye and settled on her earlobe. It was as if she was paralyzed from the neck down ,yet, somehow, she felt the warm sensation flood through her veins and slowly crawl along her left arm moments before her mind got woozy, her eyelids became heavy and her mind instantly shut down.

CHAPTER TWENTY-TWO

The television screen slowly came into focus when Alex opened her eyes. The sound was muted and short red Chinese calligraphy flashed across the bottom of the screen. A frantic news reporter appeared to be describing a scene that was playing off behind her, pointing to a stationary public bus somewhere in a city.

Alex turned her attention to her dry lips, relieved to have full sensation in her tongue and that whatever had obstructed it before was no longer there. She wiggled her toes and then her fingers, realizing she had the full use of her entire body. She spotted the intravenous drip in her hand as she slowly sat up and turned to find Sam standing with his back towards her in front of the window.

"You're up." She startled him as she spoke, her feet now dangled over the side of the bed realizing the dizziness had left her head too.

Sam swung around beaming from ear to ear when he lay eyes

on his wife. "Hey, how are you feeling?" he asked rushing over to meet her.

"How long have you been up?" Alex ignored his question when she noticed his drip had already been removed.

"A while. You should wait for the doctors to clear you first before you remove that," he commented when she picked at the tape over the needle in her hand.

"Have you seen Wang?" she asked as he helped her up, feeling surprisingly stable on her feet.

"No, but I think he was here while we were unconscious. The doctors and nurses have been in and out, mostly to check on you, but none would give me any answers without Wang's consent."

"Then you don't know that someone tried to poison us with a toxic nerve gas," Alex stated.

"Is that what happened? That explains our symptoms. Wait, how do you know that? You just woke up. Did Wang tell you that?" Suddenly confused, Sam asked several questions at once.

"He did, yes. I must have woken up when he was here at some point, but that's all I remember right now."

Alex looked around the ultra-modern hospital room which looked more like one of the research labs than an infirmary.

"We should get out of here. Where are our clothes?"

"Over there," Sam pointed his chin towards a lonely hospital trolley that stood in one corner on the opposite side of the room, "but it's pointless. I've already looked into it. The door is locked and we're under constant surveillance."

Alex instantly recalled Wang mentioning something about being under quarantine. She relayed it to Sam while her eyes trailed up to the television screen where the reporter was now even more frantic than before. Behind the female reporter, a small team of masked men in head-to-toe overalls were taping off the area that surrounded the bus while panic-stricken police officials were forcing civilians away from the scene.

"Any idea what's going on there?" Alex asked Sam who was in front of the window staring outside again.

"Not exactly, but something tells me it has to do with whatever's going on down there."

Alex joined him at the window—holding the drip bag above her head— and followed his gaze to where several television news crews had gathered outside the main entrance several stories below them. Groups of confused Infinitech employees were huddled together to one side, some of whom were being interviewed by reporters. Alex looked back at the TV screen where the white-coveralled men were removing at least a dozen dead bodies from the bus into a makeshift quarantine unit. There were women, children and several elderly people.

"They're dead," Alex exclaimed, her body cold with disgust. "They're all dead Sam."

Sam turned around and glimpsed the images on the screen

but didn't comment. He was too occupied with what was happening down below. When an image of a bright yellow triangle with a skull and crossbones appeared in the corner of the screen, Alex instantly knew what had happened.

"They were poisoned, just like us. That's what's going on there. Except they weren't as fortunate as us. Wang said his men got to us just in time." She paused as reality set in. "We could have ended up like those people. He saved us."

Sam moved away from the window and sat on the edge of his bed next to her. "I don't want to say it but I'm going to. I told you he wasn't a killer. People like him who have made it their life's work to save people don't turn around and kill for their cause."

Alex turned to Sam, holding out her hand. "Take it out," she said referring to the needle from the drip. "We need to get out of here, Sam. Wang could be in trouble and whoever poisoned and tried to kill us is responsible for killing all those civilians on the bus."

Sam didn't argue and pulled the needle from her arm. He had sensed the same.

When the couple had dressed they moved to the narrow window that ran down the middle of the door and spotted two security guards in the hallway on either side of the door.

"We need a distraction. Hang on," Sam said, hovering over one of the monitors next to her bed. After pushing a few buttons and disconnecting one of the cables, a loud alarm bleeped through the room. They had mere seconds to hide against the wall behind the door before a doctor and two nurses burst through the door and hurriedly moved to where they had propped the pillows in their beds. By the time they had caught on, Alex and Sam had already locked the door behind them and knocked both guards out before making their way to the elevator at the bottom of the sterile corridor. The elevator took too long so they set off in search of the stairs. Unlike the research floors above them, there were clear signs directing them to the emergency exit and it took hardly any effort to find it. As they burst through the door, the sound of approaching security guard's shoes noisily thumped on the metal stairwell. Sam leaned over the landing and inspected the floors below as well as above them.

"They're everywhere. Whatever is happening outside has this place crawling with security," he reported.

Deciding they had a better chance if they found another way out, the pair headed back through the door and down the corridor, stopping to snatch two doctor's coats in passing. Now in a perfect disguise they slowed their pace when several security officials rushed through the stairwell door behind them, mistaking them for medical personnel.

"Let's try the elevator again," Alex suggested as they turned back towards it, burying their noses in a folder they had stolen from the unoccupied nurses station en route.

When the elevator doors opened, two junior nurses squeezed inside just before the doors closed. Aware of the two 'doctors' in the elevator behind them, their behavior instantly transformed into a hushed exchange of words. Alex tapped one on the shoulder.

"Do you by any chance know what's going on outside?" she chanced, remembering the waiter telling them that most young people in China spoke English.

The young girl's body tensed up while she nervously clutched a folder to her chest and looked to her friend who proceeded to answer.

"Someone's been going all over China killing people with a toxic nerve gas that the police say was created here at Infinitech. Hundreds of people have already died. It's the third incident in ten days. First it was the intercity train, then the airport and now the bus in Beijing."

"Do they suspect anyone yet?" Sam asked.

"Not that we know of," the second nurse answered, "but Dr. Wang's been missing, so none of us knows what's going on. Half of the Infinitech employees can't access the building and we're not allowed to leave."

"So how do they know the toxic gas was produced here? What proof do they have?" Alex asked.

The girls shrugged their shoulders in unison. "It's just what they're saying on the news," the first nurse said, after which the second girl promptly added, "I did hear a rumor that they found lab materials at one of the scenes. Apparently they had Infinitech logos on them. Also, why else would the reporters have been outside buzzing like bees around a hive for the last two days? My friend on the tenth floor said they can't even find Xun Mao."

"Who's Xun Mao?" Sam asked, to which the girls giggled in response.

"You obviously haven't been here that long, Doctor. It's Dr. Wang's sister. She heads up all the research." The girl responded in a casually calm manner before the elevator doors opened to a large staff canteen that was bustling with Infinitech employees and the two nurses swiftly exited leaving Alex and Sam behind. Once alone and out of earshot, Sam turned to Alex.

"I guess we can safely stick to our theory of it being a full-blown corporate war."

Alex shook her head. "I'm still not sure I agree with you, Sam. I might not be as well informed as you are about these things, but a lunatic killing innocent people all across China with a deadly nerve gas doesn't sound like corporate war to me. It doesn't make sense."

"It's a simple case of corporate sabotage. Either Infinitech is behind the killings for whatever their reasons or someone's setting them up to look like they're behind them," Sam explained.

"But something doesn't add up. What's the manna got to do with anything? And the dead priest? Wang said they needed it to create some breakthrough pharmaceutical. These are chemical bombs killing people, not curing cancer." Alex repeatedly pushed the elevator button to Wang's office when the doors opened at an empty floor.

"Exactly. A rival company got wind of it, wants to sabotage their endeavor by framing them for setting off chemical bombs all over China. That way they create the breakthrough drug, save millions of lives and come off being the heroes."

Alex paced the small space in the elevator as her mind raced with unanswered questions.

"Look, I admit, it certainly sounds plausible, but it still doesn't add up. For all we know the two might have nothing to do with each other. It could just be a coincidence of events and reporters getting it wrong," Alex reasoned.

"Or the Fangs could be behind it all." Sam ventured another theory while having a turn at the elevator button.

"The Fangs might be powerful but I fail to come up with a good enough motive for them to go around killing innocent people all over China." Alex paused and glanced up at the digital floor display above their heads.

"Why can't we get past the thirty-ninth floor? Are we stuck?"

Sam's fingers triggered the button to open the doors and cautiously popped his head out. The floor was entirely deserted.

"It's three floors. Let's take the stairs."

CHAPTER TWENTY-THREE

They found the stairwell easily and since the floor was not in use at all, they had no trouble navigating their way there. The steel stairs led them to the forty-second floor where they arrived at a charcoal gray door with a biometric hand recognition panel that was hidden behind a glass pane.

Sam cursed under his breath. "This place is like Fort Knox with all their biometrics. Even if I manage to break the glass I still need someone's hand, and since this is Wang's office, I doubt it will be just anyone's."

Alex didn't respond while she stared at the security mechanism. Then suddenly she turned back and ran down the stairs.

"We'll go in through the elevator shaft," she yelled up the stairs bursting through the door when they reached the floor below Wang's office. Similar to the previous floors, they had noticed when they hurriedly made their way through the white corridor maze in search of the elevator, that the forty-first floor was also unoccupied and had not been in use.

A sudden sense of urgency propelled Alex to move faster along the corridors. Her mind flooded with the news channel's images of the murdered victims that lay beside the bus and, still very much vivid in her mind, were the heartbroken stains in Stavros' eyes. They couldn't fail him and they couldn't fail the three priests who still feared for their lives. Feeling suddenly like she couldn't breathe, she yanked the doctor's coat off and tossed it to the floor as she continued to run in the direction of the elevator. Sam followed a short distance behind her.

"This way," he directed when Alex stopped for the first time, at a crossroads.

Sam had chosen the correct hallway and they spotted the elevator doors around the next corner. As they drew closer, the body of one of Wang's private security men came into view. They paused and Alex instinctively went for her gun behind her back, only to be reminded that it had been confiscated when they first arrived. They approached the guard's body with caution, finding it bizarre that he lay face down on the floor in front of the elevator as if he had fallen forward out of it. His feet were jamming the doors and his hands were covered with odd-looking burn marks. Sam knelt down and placed his fingers below the guard's ear to feel for a pulse, but there was none. He carefully flipped the guard's body over, intrigued by the exposed flesh he spotted along his hairline, all the while hoping that his pulse might have been too weak to detect and that he might somehow still be alive. But there was no mistaking it when the guard's badly disfigured face came into view. Alex turned and looked away, horrified by the patches of rotten skin that had fallen away from his face to leave the bone visible.

"I don't think he was exposed to the nerve gas. It looks like something ate away at his face," Sam reported, immediately backing away from the corpse.

"Judging from his position I'm guessing he was running away from whoever did this to him," Alex added.

"His body's still warm. Whatever happened wasn't that long ago," Sam said.

Alex spotted the guard's firearm several feet away where she assumed it had dropped from his hand and slid down the corridor when he fell. Grabbing the weapon she helped Sam move his body before they got into the elevator. Alex checked the 9-millimeter revolver's cylinder. There were bullets in all six of the chambers. With it being their only weapon and considering they had no idea what to expect, it didn't leave much room for error. Hidden and flanked on either side of the doors they proceeded to the top floor, trying desperately to numb their pulsing heartbeats in their ears. When the elevator stopped and the doors opened they held back, pausing in anticipation of what they feared might come their way, but nothing happened. Alex gripped the gun's wooden handle and glanced at Sam before popping her head out the door. Wang's office was quiet. She adjusted her fingers, hovering her index finger over the trigger and slowly stepped out. A quick survey yielded the bodies of two more guards on the floor near Wang's desk. With her spine against the elevator she peered around each corner to where they had received the private hologram tour from Wang. There was no one there either. Satisfied they were alone she beckoned to Sam that it was safe. As with the first guard, these two were also dead, displaying identical physical injuries.

"Sam, there's blood." Alex pointed out the trail of fresh blood that ran from behind Wang's desk all along the window to the only windowless wall in the expansive room. It was roughly nine feet wide, oddly curved and symmetrically positioned between the floor-to-ceiling windows on either side. The blood stopped directly in front of it.

"That's odd. It stops dead, right here," Sam commented while he traced the droplets back to the chair behind the desk.

Alex stared at the wall, as confused as Sam was. She reached her hand out and touched it, surprised at how much it felt like the rubbery sides of a thick balloon.

"If this blood is Wang's he couldn't have just disappeared into thin air," Sam said as he made his way back along the trail.

"He didn't. There's a room or something behind here," Alex commented as her hands glided up and down the convex wall above the blood drops.

"Perhaps this is the door to the stairs," she guessed.

"Nope, that's over on the other end." Sam tapped his knuckles as he had now become accustomed to doing. "There's nothing here, Alex."

Alex dashed back to the desk and stared down at the decorative dragon painted on the desk.

"The eyes unlocked the hologram. Perhaps there's another activation here somewhere."

She traced her fingers along the dragon's swooping green tail, pausing slowly on each of the red scales, but nothing happened. She stood back, frustrated that she was wrong.

"It's got to be here somewhere," she said.

Sam had joined her at the table, now also gliding his fingers along the dragon's claws while Alex kept staring at the dragon's face. Sudden excitement washed over her when she spotted the dragon's forked tongue. It wasn't quite flush with the rest of the image displaying a shallow hollowed-out space. She allowed her fingers to rest in the cavity, tracing along the edges.

"That's it! Look, there's a piece missing here." She yanked the drawer open and searched the empty space for the missing puzzle piece but found nothing.

"He might have had it on him," Sam suggested from where he was searching the surface of the desk.

Alex didn't answer. She was on all fours under the desk, smoothing her hands along the bamboo flooring and all along the outside edges towards the front of the desk.

"Got it!" she yelled when her hand felt the almost wafer-thin, tongue-shaped two-inch piece of wood that had wedged itself between a narrow slit under one leg of the table. Shaking with excitement her hand flipped the tongue-piece over and slipped it perfectly into the painted dragon's face. As with the eyes, the mystical creature's tongue glowed a bright red and they heard the secret door slide away behind them. Expecting a hidden room on the other side of the wall, they found instead another pod elevator, much like the one they'd been in downstairs in the main reception area. The blood trail continued into the small oblong shaped pod as they stepped inside. Gazing at the single panel with three bright green logograms inside the pod, they paused.

"I have no idea what it says," Sam said, slightly tongue-in-cheek, when Alex looked to him for guidance.

"Well, here goes nothing," Alex said as she pushed the one furthest to the right.

The door responded by promptly closing before they felt the weightless motion of the elevator descending at a frightening pace. They steadied themselves but, surprisingly the speed gradually decreased before it eventually stopped. Expecting the pod to open up, it didn't and instead they remained stationary.

"They write from right to left, don't they?" Sam asked without waiting for an answer as he pushed the middle button.

The pod jerked to the left almost throwing them both off balance. This time they traveled sideways instead of vertically, as if they were in an underground train. When it finally stopped again, Alex reached out towards the last green button, taking a deep breath before she pushed it. Again the pod reacted contrary to what they expected by rotating ninety degrees before it promptly opened. Unprepared, their gaze met that of a tall slender Chinese woman dressed in a bright red, corporate suit and six-inch black heels. Her raven hair, was cut to precision in a blunt bob that extended and stopped just below her jaw, accentuating her sharp cheekbones. Beside her, Dr. Wang sat tied to a chair, forced into submission by a cylinder-shaped object resembling a futuristic looking coffee flask that was strapped to his chest. Inside, the bubble of a spirit level regulated the red liquid between two lines, visible only through a narrow transparent panel.

"I was wondering how long it would take you to get here" The woman's voice cut like the sharp blade of a sword across the room which, unlike the rest of the facility, encompassed a gray spectrum of polished walls and floors with accents of bright red. The words had barely left her mouth when Alex and Sam were faced with two QBZs aimed directly at them after which two men immediately snatched the 9-millimeter from Alex's hand. She instantly realized they were Fang members.

"You're like weeds. You just don't die. I thought for sure my nerve agent would be enough to kill you. And as predicted, my dear brother's good heart ruled his head and he jumped in to rescue you. It's always been his vice."

Alex looked at Wang's frightened face. His crisp, white silk shirt was stained with blood and the injuries to his face looked far too familiar. He had undergone the exact punishment the Fangs had inflicted on the parishioners and Khalil. The swollen bruises around his jaw suggested they'd had a fair go at breaking it with their signature beating; perhaps intentionally ceasing just in time. Disgust toward the woman pushed up from Alex's stomach and wedged in her throat, preventing her from speaking right away.

"So you're Xun Mao," she finally dared.

"You've heard of me then. How flattering?"

"Don't be. I rather wish I hadn't." Alex spoke with revulsion evident in her tone.

"Oh come on Alex. You and I are more alike than you think. Us humans are all genetically predisposed to violence. It's second nature to us."

"I'm nothing like you. I would never betray my family the way you've betrayed your brother," Alex spat back.

"Science proves otherwise, Alex. Your doctor husband would confirm it if he was honest enough. You see, it's pure biology, really. We all share a variant of the monoamine oxidase-A gene. Some call it the 'warrior gene' but if you strip the semantics, it's nothing more than your inherent will to survive. To fight for what's yours. Just like you did every time you were under attack on the boat."

CHAPTER TWENTY-FOUR

A lex felt the life drain from her face when Xun Mao's words confirmed she had indeed been the one behind all the attacks.

"You look surprised," Xun commented when she noticed Alex's shocked face. "You didn't really think this pathetic brother of mine had it in him, did you? I expected more from you, frankly. Of course it's what I want the world to think, but if the great Alex Hunt believed my charade, then so will the rest of the world."

Alex stood between the guards, her legs locked in place by the heavy feeling of contempt towards this evil woman who appeared to know everything about them. Xun casually took another sip from a rose-painted porcelain cup as if she were at a garden tea party; the motif not matching her personality at all. Contrary to Wang's softer features and ingenuous eyes, her eyes were cold and fierce, framed by thin eyebrows that arched upward at the outer corners. Her cheeks were hollowed—as if she was sucking on an invisible lollipop—

coming together at her bright red pursed lips. She displayed no emotion at all.

Alex and Sam watched as Xun swung her brother's swivel chair around to face her, careful not to disrupt the bubble gauge. Silent up till now, Wang's eyes locked with hers, but instead of displaying hatred and anger towards his sister, his eyes were filled with hurt, pity and despair.

"Why, Xun? What have I ever done to you?"

Xun's icy voice bellowed in their ears.

"Why? How laughable!" She expelled a sadistic scoff before continuing, "How long did you think I was going to continue in your shadow, Shuren? This company was mine long before you breathed your first breath. From the moment you were born I was kicked aside by our father because I was female, and you know it." She turned and placed her hands on the desk behind her, the look across her face suddenly even more rigid with resentment.

"I had nothing to do with our father's choices. I've always made you feel part of this company."

"Did you now? You certainly didn't contest his decision for you to run this company instead of me, and you definitely made sure I was stuck down here away from the world, buried under research in the labs while you paraded around like a peacock to the world. All these years, every single pharmaceutical composition created in these labs were as much my hard work as they were yours, and never once did you give me the credit."

"Is that what this is about? Acclamation? Fame?" Wang asked. "What happened to creating a better world together, Xun? Saving humanity and healing our nation? Remember that?"

Xun ignored her brother's interrogation, obviously intended to make her feel guilty. She glanced at the diamond encrusted gold watch on her arm and swiftly moved across the room to where she switched a computer's display to a large television screen directly across from Wang. Her fingers moved across the keyboard, setting into motion recorded video footage of several commuters somewhere on a train.

"Perfect timing. Why don't you two come closer?" She was referring to Alex and Sam, her voice thick with self-satisfaction. "The world is about to witness just how powerful the mighty Infinitech really is."

They had no choice when the two Fang members shoved Alex and Sam behind Wang's chair, forcing them to watch the TV screen that was suspended from the charcoal grey ceiling. A moment later the screen switched to an international news channel's studio where the presenter was reporting live on air. He paused, receiving instructions in his ear before the channel promptly switched to cellphone footage of an eighty-foot digital billboard that towered over Hong Kong's busiest cross-harbor tunnel in Hung Hom. Broadcasted on it were the commuters on the train, the exact video footage triggered by Xun's computer screen a mere five feet away from them. A red haze wafted through the train and Alex, Sam and Wang, along with millions of viewers watched in horror when, one by one, the passengers' faces melted away from their skulls before the rest of their bodies slowly liquefied until they bubbled in puddles throughout the train. Distressed civilians, sent into panic by the footage, dispersed into the street as chaos ensued. A minute later video footage of civilians in a shopping district in Shanghai flashed across the screen and once again the horror images of another chemical attack sent crowds of people fleeing from a mall.

"Stop it, Xun!" Wang yelled. "This is madness! You're killing millions of innocent people, and for what? To make me out to be a devil?"

"You still don't get it, do you?" she shouted back. "You, Infinitech and the entire hierarchy of China have taken me for granted. For years you have robbed me of my contribution to this industry and passed my hard work off as your own, just so our dearest father could boast about you to all our family and the mighty Infinitech could stay at the top. Now he's dead, and it is time the world sees who you and Infinitech really are. Once again I did the groundwork for you and you excluded me from possibly the biggest break-through in regenerative medicine by taking over. No more. All that's left for you to do is to hand over the manna's complete formula. It's the last *power* I'll ever give you. The longer you take to give me what I want, the more people will pay for it."

Alex met Sam's gaze when they simultaneously attempted to piece it all together.

"You have the manna, then?" Sam's voice broke through

Xun's ferocious attack on her brother, forcing her attention away from him.

Xun tugged the hem of her jacket in an effort to compose herself.

"He speaks after all. I was beginning to think you had no backbone Dr. Sam Quinn." She took another sip of her tea before placing it back on her desk.

"Yes, she does now. She finally got her greedy hands on it when my own security also betrayed me. Clearly I couldn't trust them either," Wang said to Xun.

"Oh come on little brother. You're not exactly innocent in all of this. You certainly seized the moment to sneak in there and steal the manna when I stupidly provided the perfect distraction for you. I did you a favor by killing that priest. No wonder you kept it hidden from everyone. Even me. We wouldn't want the world to think you're a murderer now would we? You certainly could have saved me a lot of trouble Shuren. It took me a while to figure it out, I must confess. I always thought you to be a coward, but never a thief. You must want this really badly to have stolen the manna from a church."

"I was going to tell you, Xun," Wang said.

"By working on the formula behind my back. Well, its too late. Your groundbreaking pharmaceutical will never see the light of day."

"I don't understand. What can you possibly achieve by having the manna? Clearly your mission in life is to kill and destroy. The manna brings healing, a philosophy you evidently don't even follow."

Xun rose from where she had taken a seat on the side of the desk and walked up to face Alex. She was even taller up close in her six-inch heels as she towered over her.

"Oh, you naive little thing. Do you realize the magnitude of the manna's power? For seven years I've been watching lizards grow their tails back and snails regenerate their shells, coming closer and closer to creating the world's first and only cell and tissue regenerating drug. But the formula was incomplete. We tested everything that breathed on this earth from the rarest lizards to the oldest snails on the planet and none of the chemical compounds worked. Until we heard about the miraculous liquid that's been reproducing itself for centuries, seeping from the seventeen-hundred-year-old bones of a man. All these years I've turned to insects and reptiles in my research and never once did it occur to me that the human composition is vastly different from any other species. I'm a scientist. How could I refuse something that's been right under my nose all these years?" Xun took a seat in front of her computer before her fingers moved over her keyboard once again.

Alex frowned as she tried to make sense of it all.

"Then why kill thousands of people if you intend on creating a regenerative cure to heal people?" Alex asked.

Her words instantly had Xun throw back her head in laughter.

"Because she's reverse engineering it into a weapon," Sam said in a low monotone.

"Well, look at you, Doctor. You're a lot smarter than I thought. I could have done with you on my research team," Xun mocked.

"Is that true, Xun? You want the formula to create chemical weapons. Tell me it's not true." Wang's anguished voice, bitter with disappointment, begged for his sister to deny it, but she couldn't.

"So you commissioned the Fangs to kill the priest and bully your way in to get your filthy hands on the manna," Alex said angrily.

"Commissioned them? I AM the Fangs you stupid girl. Look around you. You're in a multinational pharmaceutical company. We create drugs all day long. Why would I not seize the opportunity to make my own money from it? I'm almost sixty-five years old and I've worked under my little brother's reign my entire life. The manna is my ticket out of here."

"Then why kill the priest, hurt the parishioners and Khalil and then come after us?" Alex asked.

"Ah, the priests. All four of them fought hard to protect the manna and I had to get my message across somehow. The dead priest was the first to defy me, a fatal mistake on his part. You, on the other hand, stuck your nose where it didn't belong; a thorn in my flesh. At first I thought I could use you to get the manna for me. Until of course you somehow landed up here. I underestimated you. But, it turned out I didn't need you anyway. It wasn't that hard to get my dear brother's security to turn on him. Money has a way of doing the convincing on my behalf."

"How could you, Xun? Stop this. We can work things out. Infinitech will never survive this scandal. We'll have nothing left. You don't have to go through with this." Wang begged his sibling again.

"Oh cheer up, little brother. You won't be alive to experience the world's ridicule when I'm done anyway. I'll be halfway across the world living out my life in luxury by the time they discover your liquefied remains. I don't need you or this excuse for a company anymore."

Alex glanced down at the chemical bomb strapped to Wang's chest. If he moved he'd end up like his security team. Her eyes glanced at Xun who was once again busy on her computer. For the first time since stepping into her underground laboratory, Alex scanned her eyes around the room. It was as icy cold as its tenant. Half research lab and half executive office. Behind them the two Fang members remained in position, their guns for the moment relaxed and pointed to the ground. Her eyes met Sam's, silently agreeing to put a stop to Xun before she claimed more innocent lives through her insanity. As far as they could tell, Xun was unarmed, but so were they. Though again the Fangs' inexperience was evident as they'd neglected to restrain their hands. Distracted by her vengeance-fueled mission, with her back towards them, Xun's fingers worked the keys on her computer and Alex and Sam prepared their attack. But in that instant,

Xun's last keystroke sent another image, of a school full of young children, across the television screen.

"NO! You have to stop, Xun!" Wang screamed.

"You don't tell me what to do anymore, little brother. Give me the rest of the formula or they all die."

Wang's face displayed the absolute torture that ripped through his being. His eyes lost, searching for a way out. If he gave her the missing sequence of the formula her chemical weapons would kill millions all around the world. If he didn't, a school full of innocent children would pay the price.

"I don't have all day, Shuren. Spit it out!" Xun yelled as her patience wore thin.

"Think about what you're doing, Xun. They don't deserve it."

I'm done playing games with you, Shuren! This is your last chance. Give it to me or I kill them."

Wang no longer cried. Instead he was as calm as the sea before a storm when he spoke.

"Fine, you win. Give me a pen and pad."

Xun rose to her feet and, pen and pad in hand, walked over to her brother.

"I knew you'd come around. Like I said, you're too nice. It has always been your fallibility."

As Xun placed the pen in her brother's hand and held out the writing pad, Wang dug his heels into the floor, leaped forward in the chair and pushed his sister backwards onto her desk, crushing the toxic flask between their bodies.

And, as Shuren Wang selflessly gave his life in support of the one ideology he had always lived by, Alex and Sam disarmed their unsuspecting captors before sending them unconscious to the floor.

CHAPTER TWENTY-FIVE

Sam leaped across the floor in a futile attempt to save Wang, but it was too late. The chemical bomb had detonated and trapped the red liquid between their bodies, viciously eating away at their flesh. Still in awe of Shuren Wang's heroic act, Alex darted to the computer where the video of the school continued to play.

"We need to get those kids out of there!" she called out to Sam.

On the computer screen a large red button with a single Chinese logogram hovered across the middle of the screen. Hesitant to do anything they stared at the block.

"Leave it, Alex. Any of the keys on her keyboard could set the bomb off. Our safest bet is finding something in the video that might disclose the school's name. Perhaps we missed it earlier."

Agreeing that Sam's suggestion was the smarter option they scrutinized the TV screen, watching a dozen kids, between the ages of three and six, sitting listening to a story on the floor at their teacher's feet, oblivious to the danger that lurked in their classroom and the death threat upon their heads. Alex and Sam's eyes frantically scanned the screen for a name or logo of the school, but there was nothing.

"We don't have time for this," Alex blurted out impatiently while she turned to where the two Fang members still lay unconscious on the floor. She picked up a pistol that lay nearby and squatted next to them before her hand slapped one across the cheek. He didn't move, so she slapped him again, this time much harder, before she wrapped her fist around his collar and raised his head from the floor.

"Wake up!" she yelled, shaking him with fury.

Sam joined her, lifting the man into a sitting position when he stirred.

"Time to do something good, mate," Sam yelled at him as the mobster regained his faculties.

"Where is the school?" Alex immediately questioned him, holding the gun right up to his nose while Sam locked his arms in place behind his back.

The Fang member didn't answer. Instead, his heartless eyes remained fixed on Alex's as he challenged the threat of the gun in his face. Alex moved her face in closer, her chin almost touching her wrist while she pushed the gun firmly against the man's cheek.

"If you think I'm going to let those kids die to save your life you're making a big mistake. Either you tell me where the school is, or I take you apart, limb by limb."

The faintest flicker in the man's eyes told Alex that her threat had worked, yet the man didn't respond, calling her bluff. She moved the gun over his kneecap while her threatening eyes remained on his and firmly pushed the gun down into his knee.

"Okay, okay!" The man surrendered quickly. "It's a school in Chongqing."

"What's its name?" Sam said close to his ear.

"Ying Zheng."

"How far is it from here?" Alex asked.

The mobster let out a half-suppressed laugh and Alex responded by pushing the gun into his kneecap again. The threat yanked him back to reality.

"You can't get there, okay. It's too far. It's at least fifteen hours by train."

Frustrated, Alex pushed him against the floor and rose to her feet. She paced back and forth in front of him as her mind tried to plan their next move. Out of time and out of patience she stopped midway and pushed the gun back in his face.

"How did she plant the bomb?"

"Ah come on, man. The Fangs don't tolerate traitors. I'm dead if I tell you."

"You're dead anyway, now tell me how she planted the bomb."

The man swore in his native tongue.

"It was planted by a Fang member from the area."

Alex gathered her thoughts before she leaped back to Xun's desk in search of the woman's phone. Snatching it off the desk she crossed the room to where Xun's disfigured body was pinned under Wang's.

"Don't touch her, Alex!" Sam warned when Alex reached out to lift Xun's arm.

Alex heeded Sam's warning and, without touching Xun, hovered the phone below her thumb. It worked and instantly the phone unlocked.

Alex was back with the mobster on the floor.

"You're going to call your scumbag friend from her phone and tell him to disarm and remove the bomb. Tell him Xun ordered you to call him. Not a word about her death. Got it?"

She pushed the phone in front of his face, waiting for him to direct her through the contacts list on the phone. A moment later the dial tone cut through the tense atmosphere. Sam tightened his grip on the gangster's arms while Alex pushed the gun's barrel into the man's shoulder just above his collar-bone, warning him not to chance anything.

A man on the other end of the call answered, and Alex moved the tip of her gun to the spot between the guard's eyes. From her harsh stare it was evident she wasn't playing around and he promptly responded to her threat with a short exchange in Mandarin. The man on the other end's tone elevated a few notches, signifying he wasn't in agreement, and caused Alex to apply more pressure to the gun. The gangster's voice argued back in response, knowing he needed to convince his friend or he'd lose his life. Whatever he said worked and, a moment later, the one on the other end switched the phone off.

"Talk," Alex commanded.

"He's at the school. He was waiting on Xun's orders to go ahead. He's on his way back in."

Alex turned and watched the video on the television screen, seeing a heavily tattooed man with a gun enter the classroom and move past the educator, sending her into total panic while she huddled the children in a corner. The man ignored them and casually pulled a chair against the wall, onto which he then climbed in order to reach the ventilation duct above his head. His hands reached in and slowly removed a cylindrical container almost identical to the one Wang had had pinned around his chest except this one had a cellphone attached to it instead of a spirit level. A swift but cautious move of his fingers disconnected the phone, after which he placed the cylinder inside a silver case in his small backpack before leaving as casually as he had entered.

"Satisfied?" the man under Alex's aim said with disdain.

Sam responded by pulling his arms back against their joints, causing the Fang member to squirm with pain.

"Are there more?" Sam's tone was harsh.

"No," the man moaned in reply.

"Where's the manna?" Sam continued.

"I don't know."

"Come on! You really think we're going to believe you after you've spent hours at this woman's side?" Alex called him out.

"It's the truth. I don't know where it is," the man responded; his attention held firm under gunpoint.

Alex swung the back of her gun across his cheek, sending the gangster back into unconsciousness. He was of no use to them anymore. Finally able to let go of the mobster, Sam dropped his body to the floor.

Alex allowed her eyes to scan the room. Sam did the same.

"It's got to be here somewhere. I can't imagine she'd have left it upstairs in one of the labs." Alex thought out loud while she slowly moved through the room.

"My old man always says it takes a thief to catch a thief. We need to get inside her head," Sam suggested, as he rummaged through the vials on her laboratory table.

"Spare me! She's a cold-hearted killer who sought nothing but acclaim and money. All she cared about was herself, even to the point where she betrayed and killed her own flesh and blood. It's despicable."

Sam closed the door of a small incubator and turned to face Alex.

"All I'm saying is that she was a scientist. Scientists are convergent thinkers as opposed to most people who are divergent, like us."

Alex was back at Xun's desk, staring at it in the hope that her eyes would find a clue.

"I have no idea what that even means, Sam. All I know is that she had the manna and that she'd have hidden it somewhere out of sight, considering it formed the cornerstone of her discovery. Wang's office operated with the dragon. She might have something similar."

"See, that's my point exactly," Sam said.

"What? Sam we don't have time for this," Alex snapped.

"Xun and Wang couldn't have been more different. Polar opposites. He was creative, a divergent thinker while she on the other hand, was analytical, logical, a convergent thinker. She'd have hidden it in a logical place. Like a safe," Sam explained, from where he now stood over the remains of her body.

"Okay, assuming your theory is correct, where would her safe be? I don't see anything that looks like a safe or anywhere she'd conceal one. There's not even one single picture on the wall, nothing."

Sam sat down at Xun's computer desk, slowly skimming his eyes over the objects on the surface.

"Unless she hid it in plain sight. How genius?" Sam said

triumphantly as his hand moved to a thermos flask directly in front of him. The steel object was cold to the touch.

"She was drinking a cup of tea," Alex noted, shoving her hands into her pants' pockets.

"Indeed, but wouldn't the tea flask be hot? This is as cold as ice."

"Only one way of finding out." Alex encouraged Sam, who didn't hesitate to unscrew the cup off the top.

"Interesting," Sam remarked as he stared down at the bright red electronic lock on the flask's lid. "It appears we require a password."

A grid of twelve small Chinese calligraphy squares glowed against the stark black background of the thermos' lid. Apart from the asterisk and the hashtag sign, they couldn't interpret any of the other ten.

"It has to be numbers, right?" Alex asked Sam

"I'd assume so, yes."

"She was a Fang. Let's try forty-nine."

"And how are we supposed to do that when neither of us can read or write Chinese?" Sam said playfully.

Alex fell quiet.

"There! In the school," she yelled out when a poster on the wall displayed a bilingual number chart.

Sam's fingers copied the numbers across, pressing the hashtag at the end. Nothing happened. He tried again, this time without the hashtag, but again nothing happened.

Alex started pacing the space behind him.

"She might have had a different number. It was an identifier, perhaps they're hierarchical and her identifier was different."

She dashed over to Xun's body and used a pen to lift the watch away from her wrist. Cursing under her breath when she recognized the identical markings as with the other Fang members, she moved back into position next to Sam.

"We're missing something," she said in frustration as she sat next to him on the desk and dug her hands back into her pockets. Her fingers touched the now familiar patch of fabric. Distracted by her efforts to figure out the numeric password she rubbed the fabric between her fingers much like she'd been doing since they found it. While deep in thought it suddenly hit her.

"She was a scientist, right? And how do scientists communicate?"

Sam shrugged his shoulders.

"Through chemical elements, the periodic table and scientific jargon. The manna is a liquid, like water—the water of life—and water is otherwise known as H_2O."

"Yes, but we're looking for numbers, not alphabetic letters, besides, water doesn't consist of a single element so it's not on the periodic table."

"True, but water is made up of hydrogen and oxygen." She paused, allowing Sam to finish her sentence.

"And those are chemical elements with atomic numbers. Alex you're a genius."

"Not quite. That's as far as my knowledge of science goes. You're the one with the degree. Do you know what their atomic numbers are?

Sam placed his palms on his temples as if he wanted to squeeze his brain into recalling the numbers.

"I think it's one for hydrogen and eight for oxygen," he eventually said.

Alex tracked it on the school poster while Sam copied it across and a split second later the red screen turned green to mark their success.

With their hearts pounding hard against their chests, Sam twisted the lid off the flask and pulled out a glass cylinder containing the cloudy liquid extracted from the bones of Saint Nick.

CHAPTER TWENTY-SIX

The hot white powdery sand forced its way into their shoes and in between their toes as Alex and Sam walked along the winding road to the blue and white taverna on the hill in Mathraki. Alex recalled the last time they had walked the path with Stavros and how crushed he was when all he had risked to save his mother turned futile in a blink of an eye. She wished with all her heart that they could have reached the island sooner, before his life changed forever.

Alex threw a sideways glance at where Khalil silently walked beside them. The bruises on his face and body remained prominent as did the braces that held his jaw in place, and whilst the sounds from his mouth were nothing but unrecognizable mumblings for the most part, they somehow knew exactly where his heart was at. At the core of his courage and humility lay a man whose own heart had been broken and who'd fought his own sorrow. A loss no man should ever have to endure.

As they neared the top of the hill, the recognizable blue

window shutters of the taverna came into view against the majestic backdrop of the Adriatic. But unlike the quiet surroundings that had welcomed them to the island the first time, they were instead greeted by blaring traditional Greek folk music intermingled with cheers of laughter that bellowed across the dunes around them.

"Well that certainly sounds festive," Sam said. "Seems we're in time for a party."

"Let's hope Doudous is in a better mood so we won't get thrown out of his restaurant again," Alex giggled as the trio walked through the taverna's front door.

Inside, the mood was far removed from that of their last visit, something Alex gladly welcomed. Her eyes searched for Stavros through the fully occupied restaurant where groups of locals were singing and dancing to the festive melodies of an accordion while they joyfully smashed dozens of plates to the floor. A long table draped in a crisp white tablecloth with dozens of delectable traditional dishes stood out of the way along one wall, seemingly the gathering place for the younger crowd. It was nearly impossible not to be swept up by the jubilant atmosphere that surrounded them. As the mingled aromas of fish, lemons and barbecue smoke drifted through the open windows on the tailcoat of the fresh sea breeze, Sam found Stavros on the other side of the taverna where he was surrounded by several motherly women. Wearing a light blue dress shirt and thin black tie his dapper look made him almost unrecognizable. Moments later Doudous burst through the kitchen door pushing a four-tiered birthday cake, illuminated by sixteen flickering candles, on a small trolley. While the partygoers clapped and cheered, and the accordion's music transformed into a celebratory tune, they watched as Stavros blew out the sixteen candles on his birthday cake.

"How about that?" Sam smiled. "It's our boy's sixteenth birthday today. Something tells me his mother had a lot to do with bringing us here today. I cannot imagine a better gift for the lad. Shall we?" Sam nudged Alex and Khalil toward Stavros whose face lit up the moment he spotted them.

"Happy Birthday, Stavros," Sam wished him first when the boy's arms flung around him in joyous embrace.

"We brought you a little gift," Alex announced and slipped her hand into her satchel to retrieve a small red box wrapped in a big white ribbon.

Stavros said something in Greek they couldn't understand but assumed to be expressing his surprise.

"Go on, open it," Sam encouraged as Doudous and his wife suddenly appeared by his side.

Hastily Stavros untied the bow and as the white ribbon fell to the floor and Stavros lifted the lid off the box, his face instantly declared what the gift meant to him. As his eyes settled on the hand-sized antique glass carafe with its decorative pewter covering, it took every bit of restraint to contain the emotions that flooded Alex's insides. And although they knew the manna wouldn't bring his mother back to life, it was, at the very least, a reminder of his courage and that he had done everything he could to save her.

As if to remind him not to linger on his sorrow, his mother's invisible spirit intervened when a group of sprightly men and women yanked Alex and Sam into their folk-dancing circle.

"No-no, I don't dance." Alex attempted to stop a man from pulling her into the circle, but the man ignored her and she found herself forced to bounce up and down along with a ring of cheerful Greeks who wouldn't take no for an answer.

Once Alex finally surrendered, the dance steps became easier, and both her and Sam settled into the rapid rhythms of the *Sirtaki*. It wasn't long before Stavros and his newfound family joined in and Alex found herself slowly letting go of the world and all the troubles that surrounded her.

The ALEX HUNT Adventures continue in The CAIAPHAS CODE. Available in eBook and Paperback **(https://books2read.com/Caiaphas-Code)**

A murder leads to the discovery of an ancient religious artifact and present-day terror. To solve the case means death!

When a determined assault on two students leaves one of them dead and the other missing near Jerusalem's famous Old City, the hunt for the killer hints on something far more sinister behind the slaying.

When the clues point to it being linked to a religious artifact of an ancient coded keepsake dating back to 36 AD, they call renowned artifact recovery specialists Alex and Sam in to help.

But they soon realize a powerful enemy behind the carefully planned plot will have them fight to decipher the code first.

Follow the infamous team between the ancient structures in and around Jerusalem, and then to Crete as the clues unravel themselves and they make a remarkable discovery so vital to history that it shakes the very core of Biblical prophecy.

Murder mystery meets riveting archaeological adventure thriller in the sixth page-turning book in the Alex Hunt Adventure Thriller series.

Inspired by true historical facts and events.
Also suitable as a standalone novel.

*Includes Bonus content and a free digital copy of the series prequel.

Receive a FREE copy of the prequel and see where it all started!

NOT AVAILABLE ANYWHERE ELSE!

Click on image or enter http://download.urcelia.com in your browser

MORE BOOKS BY URCELIA TEIXEIRA

ALEX HUNT Adventure Thrillers

Also suited as standalone novels

The PAPUA INCIDENT - Prequel (sign up to get it FREE)

The RHAPTA KEY

The GILDED TREASON

The ALPHA STRAIN

The DAUPHIN DECEPTION

The BARI BONES

The CAIAPHAS CODE

FREE BONUS - BEHIND THE BOOK

DOWNLOAD AN EXCLUSIVE BEHIND THE BARI BONES BOOKLET

Over 60 pages of additional links, images and information on St. Nicholas, the setting, weapons used, character visualization, and much more!

Click image and download or type in http://bit.ly/ Behind-Bari-Bones in your browser.

If you enjoyed this book, I would sincerely appreciate it if you could take the time to **leave a review**. It would mean so much to me!

For sneak previews, free books and more,

Join my mailing list

No-Spam Newsletter
ELITE SQUAD

FOLLOW Urcelia Teixeira

BookBub has a New Release Alert. Not only can you check out the latest deals, but you can also get an email when I release my next book by following me here

https://www.bookbub.com/authors/urcelia-teixeira

Website:
https://www.urcelia.com

Facebook:
https://www.facebook.com/urceliabooks

Twitter:
https//www.twitter.com/UrceliaTeixeira

ABOUT THE AUTHOR

Urcelia Teixeira is an author of fast-paced archaeological action-adventure novels with a Christian nuance.

Her Alex Hunt Adventure Thriller Series has been described by readers as 'Indiana Jones meets Lara Croft with a twist of Bourne'. She read her first book when she was four and wrote her first poem when she was seven. And though she lived vicariously through books, and her far too few travels, life happened. She married the man of her dreams and birthed three boys (and added two dogs, a cat, three chickens, and some goldfish!) So, life became all about settling down and providing a means to an end. She climbed the corporate ladder, exercised her entrepreneurial flair and made her mark in real estate.

Traveling and exploring the world made space for child-friendly annual family holidays by the sea. The ones where she succumbed to building sandcastles and barely got past reading the first five pages of a book. And on the odd occasion she managed to read fast enough to page eight, she was confronted with a moral dilemma as the umpteenth expletive forced its way off just about every page!

But by divine intervention, upon her return from yet another male-dominated camping trip, when fifty knocked hard and fast on her door, and she could no longer stomach the profanities in her reading material, she drew a line in the sand and bravely set off to create a new adventure!

It was in the dark, quiet whispers of the night, well past midnight late in the year 2017, that Alex Hunt was born.

Her philosophy

From her pen flow action-packed adventures for the armchair traveler who enjoys a thrilling escape. Devoid of the usual profanity and obscenities, she incorporates real-life historical relics and mysteries from exciting places all over the world. She aims to kidnap her reader from the mundane and plunge them into feel-good riddle-solving quests filled with danger, sabotage, and mystery!

For more visit www.urcelia.com or email her on books@urcelia.com

facebook.com/urceliateixeira

twitter.com/urcelia_teixeira

instagram.com/urceliateixeira

DISCLAIMER & COPYRIGHT